dead ink

– Liverpool –
MMXXV

Writing the Magic

dead ink

First published in Great Britain in 2025 by Dead Ink, an imprint of Cinder House Publishing Limited.

Print ISBN: 978-1-915368-94-2
ePub ISBN: 978-1-915368-95-9
Kindle ISBN: 978-1-915368-96-6

Cover design by Luke Bird / lukebird.co.uk
Typeset by Laura Jones-Rivera / lauraflojo.com

Printed and bound in Great Britain by Clays Ltd, Elcograf S.p.A.

www.deadinkbooks.com

Writing the Magic

Essays on Crafting Fantasy Fiction

Edited by
Dan Coxon & Richard V. Hirst

dead ink

Contents

Introduction

There's a convincing argument to be made that, of all genres, fantasy is perhaps the oldest. Much of the earliest known literature features gods, monsters and magical transformations, and although other modes of writing subsequently emerged – such as realism, crime fiction, the Gothic and science fiction – these developed in response to historical shifts. Fantasy, however, has endured, evolving and adapting, yet remaining constant. Dating back as far as the *Epic of Gilgamesh* (c.2100 BCE) and Apuleius' *The Golden Ass*, this mode of writing can be traced through *Le Morte d'Arthur* and William Morris's *The Well at the World's End* to its modern-day incarnation. Neither is it a purely Western phenomenon – almost every cultural tradition contains stories of fairy tale and myth. Hindu epics like *The Ramayana*, Chinese tales of the Immortals, and the trickster myths of Indigenous cultures form the widespread roots of today's fantasy scene. Fantasy, at its purest, offers an act of imaginative creation that feels fundamental to human experience.

It's little wonder, then, that many of us first encounter fantasy fiction in childhood. For those of us who discovered reading in the 1970s, 1980s and 1990s, the likes of Alan Garner, Susan Cooper and Ursula K. Le Guin proved to be formative figures, our imaginations fired by their depictions of shadowy parallel worlds, their heroes and heroines often only children themselves. Prior to this, the inter- and postwar years gave us the likes of *Mary Poppins*, *The Sword in the Stone* and *The Chronicles of Narnia*. These, likewise, were preceded by E. Nesbit's stories of magical encounters in otherwise realistic Edwardian settings; *Alice's Adventures in Wonderland*, which defied Victorian logic; and, in the eras before these, tales collected by the likes of Jacob and Wilhelm Grimm, Charles Perrault, and Madame d'Aulnoy, these stories in turn having existed for untold centuries as fireside tales.

Even a cursory glance at the shelves of YA novels in your local bookshop will show that this tradition is ongoing, and is perhaps even stronger than ever. To a young reader, there's nothing more thrilling than the possibility that there might be magical lands to explore, filled with danger and treasure and excitement.

When we enter adulthood it may be tempting to put away childish things, but fantasy is something we never truly outgrow. That sense of wonder we first experience in childhood continues to exert its sway over countless adult readers, perhaps because fantasy is a genre which still has plenty to offer – in particular, an ability to traverse the darker undercurrents of society and the realms of the human subconscious. Michael Moorcock explored the concept of the antihero through multiple novels (and multiple series of novels) in the 1970s and 1980s, and his influence is still widely seen today. Fantasy offers readers an opportunity for readers to engage most fulsomely with the strange and surreal, too, as seen in modern writers like B. Catling and Jeff VanderMeer.

Then there are the classics of the genre, those books that – much like the stories they tell – seem set to endure for several lifetimes. Amidst the effects-laden films and tie-in merch, it's easy to forget that Tolkien's *Lord of the Rings* trilogy was first published in the 1950s, in the wake of two world wars. Lewis Carroll and C.S. Lewis loom large, too, with their nascent portal fantasies hinting at other worlds sitting tantalisingly within reach. Reading such timeless works often prompts the question: is what decides whether a fantasy novel endures the way it speaks to our universal desires and anxieties? Or is it something else, with these stories connecting with an older, deeper part of human culture, something pre-verbal or instinctive?

If anything, the fantasy genre sometimes falls foul of its own popularity. In the early 1980s there was an explosion of epic fantasy in popular culture, from Fighting Fantasy's choose-your-own-adventure books to Hollywood films like *Dragonslayer*, *Krull* and Jim Henson's Muppets-noir epic *The Dark Crystal*. We're seeing a similar explosion now, following the popularity of *Game of Thrones* – and when the marketplace is flooded with imitations and hastily-scrawled derivatives, it can be hard to find the gems in the dragon's hoard. As Michael Moorcock wrote in his 1987 study of the genre, *Wizardry and Wild Romance*: 'Most of them are simply bad, several show promise, one or two are by writers of genuinely original talent.'

So how can we spot these works of 'genuine talent'? And more importantly, how can we make sure that our own work doesn't fall into the category of the 'simply bad'?

Hopefully this book can help answer those questions, and more besides. As with the three previous titles in this series – *Writing the Uncanny, Writing the Future*, and *Writing the Murder* – we've tracked down some of the most exciting writers working in the genre today, to ask them for their experience and advice. More than just a 'how to' manual, *Writing the Magic* offers you new pathways to head down – and new treasures to uncover – as you embark on your own choose-your-own-adventure as a writer.

As with all good fantasy quests, finding your travelling companions is half the battle. Francesco Dimitri opens with a rallying call to all writers of fantasy, exploring the concept of 'magic' and how we might best present it in a fictional world. RJ Barker then offers some advice (and a confession) in 'You Do Not Need to Know How to Write a Book (Or How to Embrace Ignorance and Run With It)', before Kritika H. Rao examines the role of voice in fantasy fiction, and how best to find our own authentic selves. We then turn our gaze on the best ways to build a fantasy world, with three different perspectives from Jen Williams, Jeff Noon and Alex Pheby. All three tackle world-building in strikingly unique ways, and their approaches prove (if proof is needed) that there are multiple paths leading to the same goal. Finally, we look at the use of tradition and subgenre, with Hannah Kaner making a strong case for subverting the traditional Hero's Journey narrative. Charlotte Bond then examines the long, strange history of dragons, followed by an enlightening essay by Richard Strachan on his experiences writing for Warhammer's Black Library and the challenges of playing within someone else's sandbox. Finally, Katherine

Langrish tackles fantasy in children's literature and its importance not just to those starting out on their reading journey, but to all of us as adults too.

In between there are spotlight pieces on three of the cornerstones of modern fantasy – J.R.R. Tolkien, Michael Moorcock and Ursula K. Le Guin – scribed by the expert hands of Juliet E. McKenna, J.L. Worrad and Lucy Holland. Each offers valuable insights not only into their subject, but also into the advice and lessons we can learn from these masters of the genre.

Fantasy isn't simply a literary tradition – it's a mode of thought that predates written history. Long before novels existed, there were people telling stories of peril and magic around fire-lit gatherings. Fantasy fiction continues the long and illustrious history of this mode of thought, and it shows no signs of ending. With increasingly diverse stories coming to the fore, from such talents as N.K. Jemisin, Nnedi Okorafor and Tasha Suri, the genre is still evolving and widening its borders. Whether you're a fan of epic fantasy or an explorer in the strange realms of the human psyche, hopefully this book can act as a torch to light your way, both as a reader and a writer. Then something Tookish will wake inside of you, and you'll feel the urge to have an adventure…

Starting the Journey

As with all great adventures, writing fantasy fiction often begins with a single step. Are you driven by the stories you want to tell, or enthused by the world you're starting to imagine? Have your characters taken on a life of their own, to the extent that *they* are the ones writing their story?

Here you'll find three starting points for your writing quest, from three authors who have walked these paths many times before. Whether you're trying to discover your own unique voice or working out how you want to present your fantasy world – or, indeed, are simply asking yourself why you want to write at all – these perspectives offer you a map to navigate by.

So why not pick up a pen and a sheet of paper (or maybe a scroll), and let the adventure begin...

Words of Magic

Francesco Dimitri

I finally got my hands on *The Lord of the Rings* when my parents brought me to Pisa, not to see the leaning tower, but for a medical check-up. It went well. To celebrate, I asked to visit my favourite kind of place – a bookshop. There was no shortage of books in our home: my maternal grandfather was an SF enthusiast, my father loved comics, and my mother read poetry and all the classics. Bookshops, though, were another matter.

This was 1991, and we lived in a small town in southern Italy. Browsing for books meant visiting a shop and physically going through whatever books the owner had decided to put on their shelves. By and large, you were stuck with somebody else's picks. My hometown boasts two bookshops now; at the time, the closest one was a forty-five-minute drive away. They did not have *The Lord of the Rings*.

It was not a popular pick. In Italy, for a series of ridiculous reasons, *The Lord of the Rings* had long been considered a fascist-adjacent book, and many booksellers, well, they just did not stock it. Also, it featured magic. The upper classes were not supposed to read books with magic, and the lower ones were not supposed to read books at all.

Like all children and most sensible adults, I didn't mind all that. What I cared about was to see what happened to Bilbo Baggins after he got back to the Shire. My reading diet was broad, though tilting towards the magical and the fantastic. Up to that point, my drugs of choice had been Angela Sommer-Bodenburg's *The Little Vampire* series, the *Choose Your Own Adventure* books, the Sherlock Holmes stories, and the Sandokan novels (a hugely popular Italian series about Asian pirates fighting European empires). I considered *The Neverending Story* my favourite book; *The Hobbit*, which I had read recently, had come surprisingly close. I had heard that *The Lord of The Rings* was more challenging, more adult. I was ten. Of course I wanted it.

I am pretty sure my parents would have phoned some shop and ordered it for my next birthday if I kept pestering them, but there was no need. In that bookshop in Pisa, I finally found my grail. It was large, and heavy, and solemn-looking. When I put my hands on it, a celestial music played in my ears.

Only, the bookseller didn't mean to hand it to me. 'You're too little,' she said. 'And the book is too big.' She was not even concerned it was too difficult; no, she was concerned it was *too big*. It had never occurred to me that weight could be a unit of measurement for books. To cut her some slack, this one was expensive, and she was probably trying to spare my parents some money. They could buy a *Little Vampire* book for a lot less and they would be sure that I would get to the end of it. But I had had a medical check-up which had turned out okay. I was, briefly, the master of my own destiny.

So, I went back home dragging a volume which was almost as tall as myself. I swore I would read it from cover to cover; if nothing else, to spite that stranger who thought I couldn't.

I spent the next five months doing just that, and letting that book change my life. Everything I have done since was heavily influenced by those five months. My love for mushrooms comes from the hobbits. I wanted to visit England because it was the closest I could get to the Shire, and here I am, living in London. I was not struck by light on the way to Damascus; I was struck by words while I was reading in my usual position, sitting on my bed, with my legs leaning upwards on the wall (children are weird). The book spoke to me in a thousand ways, big and small. Some big parts of the story spoke to me in small ways (I could take or leave the battles), and some small parts spoke to me in big ways (Tom Bombadil!). One of the details that stayed with me is relevant to the point I'm getting to.

When Sam starts on the journey, he does not do that to save the world, or to look after Frodo, or to chase after fame and fortune. He leaves his home behind and ventures into the great unknown for no better reason than because he wants to see the elves. 'I do love tales of that sort,' he says. 'And I believe them too.'

That resonated with me to an extent that a ten-year-old could not quite articulate. Only decades later did I realise that it was the one compass I had been following through all my life, in my reading as well as in my writing, as well as in any choice that mattered. Every single book I bought and every single book I wrote and every single life-changing decision I made, I did it because, like Sam, I wanted to see the elves. I wanted more than a good life. I wanted a good story; I wanted magic.

* * *

The oldest story ever told by humans – or the oldest which survived, anyway – is a story of magic. It comes from Mesopotamia, the land between the rivers Tigris and Euphrates, where writing was first developed and history as such begun. It tells the adventures of Gilgamesh, a great king of semi-divine ancestry who tries and fails to become immortal. Though more than four thousand years old, the story has aged splendidly: with its prophetic dreams, spectacular spells and heroic characters, it has all the trappings of a blockbuster. It features the first magic circle in history. Before Dennis Wheatley, before the Dresden files, before *Buffy*, there was *Gilgamesh*. Still, it is not what we would call 'fantasy'.

This is not me nitpicking about genre – well, not only. This is about the crucial matter of how we see the world and how we decide to move through it. When we read fantasy, we take for granted that we are going to find in the story elements which do not belong to the real world: even at ten years old, I knew there was little chance I would get to see any elves in the flesh. But within the mindset of the people who told the story of Gilgamesh, no element of that story was necessarily unreal. In the Mesopotamia of four millennia ago, mortals were dealing with spirits all the time, and spells were a component of state-craft. The other early mention of a magic circle comes from the same area, and it is found in an inscription chronicling the acts of a historical king. Magic circles were a fact of life, and so were gods and demons. Strictly speaking, 'magic' did not exist yet, not in any way we could recognise (we will have to wait until the Greeks for that). There was no clear-cut difference between what we call magic and what we call religion, science, philosophy, politics. That was because, at a more fundamental level, there was no difference between the 'natural' and the 'supernatural'. Nature was full of spirits and hidden powers, and it was only sensible to find ways to work with them. The epic of Gilgamesh was to its tellers as much of a fantasy story as Stendhal's *Le Rouge et Le Noir* (another tale about a man trying and failing to rise above his station) was to the French of the nineteenth century.

It is not for me to say if Ancient Mesopotamians were factually right or wrong. I don't think it is for anybody to say: I am deeply suspicious of anyone, priest or scientist, who has some ultimate truth to peddle. But there is a common idea we would do well to get rid of: the idea that cultures which regularly deal with the invisible world don't know any better; the idea that psychiatric drugs cast out demons better than any exorcism. The idea, in other words, that magic is for those who cannot do science yet.

There is, to be sure, a grain of truth in that. When I read a translation of a Mesopotamian tablet suggesting you can heal an illness by dragging a goat into the sick person's bed,

I feel very grateful for doctors. Statistics are probably a better prognostication tool than haruspicy, which requires us to slay an animal and read fortunes in their entrails. The trajectory of science has given us marvels, and opportunities for health and wealth never before seen in history. That said, it is one trajectory among many, and when we decide to live by only one trajectory, only one truth, we invariably lose more than we gain. We contain multitudes. We can accept the value of what we can touch and measure, and still dream of more.

In our culture, we tend to believe that only humans are fully alive, while the rest of the world is mindless matters to shape (to exploit, or to save, but anyway to control). There is another way of looking at things, which sees the rest of the world as a living, breathing organism, a character in its own right. For hundreds of thousands of years, and until only a few centuries ago, this 'magical' mindset was shared by humanity as a whole.

It never went away, not entirely. There will always be a part of us which hears voices in the wind, and in the split-second before we move on, wonders – what if they had something to say?

This is the root of fantasy.

* * *

Each and every human who ever lived has felt, at some point in their life, a sense of what we came to call *the supernatural*; a sense of another world touching ours. When you were a kid and you were afraid of the dark, not because there could be strangers, but because the dark might have tentacles; when you saw an impossible shape from the corner of your eye; when you smelt your grandma's perfume in your room, on the night your grandma passed away in another city; when you felt you were not alone, while you should, in fact, be alone in your house; when you thought you saw your reflection in the mirror grin at you; maybe even now, when you feel a prickle on the back of your neck and an urge to turn and see whether someone is watching you – that is the feeling of the supernatural at play.

Some of us will find a rational explanation for that feeling. Like Scrooge in *A Christmas Carol*, some of us will think that their experience was 'an undigested bit of beef, a blot of mustard, a crumb of cheese, a fragment of underdone potato'. The minds of others will run to ghosts and curses and *Cthulhu fhtagn*. Others yet will suspend their judgement. And the especially unimaginative ones will just shrug and go on with their chores.

But the feeling itself was real. Whatever you want to make of it, however you decide to box it in your mind, you went through an experience, a moment you could not immediately accommodate within the humdrum reality that is familiar to you. This kind of experience is even more fundamental than love or hatred. It sits at the same basic level as attraction and disgust, fear and hope. It belongs to the animal that is *Homo sapiens*.

We went on to acquire a lot more power than any other animal on this planet – though we have no idea whether that is good for us, or bad, or just another thing (it is entirely possible that ravens have, on average, a better time than humans, and that an octopus's short life is filled with an alien meaning we cannot begin to grasp). Be that as it may, we acquired that power through technology – but buried beneath our shiny toys, our fundamental nature remains. We have hands which are as good at making tools as they are at punching other *sapiens* in the face. We have teeth made for slashing and lips made for sucking. We act like fools because we want to mate with a specific someone. And sometimes, we hear voices in the wind.

We know little about what humans were up to back in the early days of our species, but we do know something. We know, for example, that even before *Homo sapiens* came onto the world stage, there was another human species, *Homo neanderthalensis*, which would bury their dead in ways which did not make any pragmatic sense. About 350,000–400,000 years ago, Neanderthals were journeying to the bottom of a deep cave in Atapuerca, Spain, to bury bodies, possibly singing and making music in the process (this is an almost inconceivably long time: if we walked one mile a year for 400,000 years, we could get to the moon and back). They would carry a dead person into the belly of the earth, trekking a long way down, leaving behind every hope of natural light, using intensely scented torches which had taken time and effort to produce, just to make sure they would rest a body in a specific spot. It would be easier to just bury their dead or leave them to be eaten by animals – but no, they decided to put them there and not anywhere else. They were thinking beyond the concerns of the here and now. They were thinking of another world, and that other world mattered to them, a lot.

We know that 40,000 years ago, during the last Ice Age, some *Homo sapiens* were carving the sculpture of a lion-man in a mammoth tusk, which is a difficult material to carve. The job must have taken around four hundred hours, which would be a lot of time today, but it was an order of magnitude more so in an age where every single calorie was needed to survive, and humans had to hunt and gather every day for those calories. From a strictly rational perspective, they could have used those four hundred hours to do something better than create an image of a being which did not exist. And they never stopped acting like that. Around 20,000 years later, they were drawing figures on the walls of deep caves in France and Spain. Again, it did not make much sense, rationally, for them to spend so much time and effort to decorate walls of places in which they did not even live.

Our best hypothesis is that the Lion-man and the images in the caves were both used for ritual purposes – which is a non-committal way of saying that they were used to work magic. These early humans were already experiencing something that went beyond mundane concerns, even at a time when mundane concerns were literally a matter of life and death. An attraction to magic, the feeling that there is more to the world than it seems, is not the idle fantasy of a people who grew too comfortable for their own good, but rather, it is one of the features that make us *people* in the first place.

Cyclically throughout history, magic has been declared dead; and invariably, the reports of its death were greatly exaggerated. The first Christians said their religion had vanquished magic: all magicians would kneel at the feet of baby Jesus, bringing him gifts and recognising that after his birth, their craft had been superseded. It turned out this was just propaganda. Centuries later, it was the turn of Enlightenment philosophers, who said their discoveries had made magic obsolete – while alchemy flourished and people invoked demons. In the early twentieth century, sociologist Max Weber said that science had brought about a 'disenchantment of the world', but already a new wave of occultism was sweeping through France and the UK. Lenin created a materialistic State, but after his death, his body was mummified and preserved in a mausoleum, and legends were told that he would rise by night to roam the land.

A thirst for magic is deeply ingrained within the human psyche. It needed to find a voice in the rough early days of our species, it needed to find a voice as soon as we invented writing, it needed to find a voice while we were coming up with the very idea of science. And it needs to find a voice here and now.

It would be tempting to say that this is what fantasy books are for; but it is not so simple.

* * *

That fantasy books are full of magic is a truism: even the 'low-magic' ones are defined by it, if only by virtue of its comparative scarcity. But a question worth asking – a question I have been asking for most of my life as a reader, and all of my life as a writer – is: *why magic?* What is magic for, in a book?

In most cases I can think of, magic is flavouring, window-dressing. It is not a fundamental component of the story. Take

Charlaine Harris's Southern Vampire Mysteries. I came to the books after watching the series they inspired, *True Blood*. They are fast and furious fun, not life-changing, but satisfying in the way a cold beer and grilled shrimp are satisfying on a hot summer's night. They feature vampires, werewolves, witches, fairies and whatnot, who kill and/or fuck each other abundantly. The books are saying something about small-town life (which Harris depicts more realistically than many of my friends born and bred in cities realise), about lust, even fear. But there is very little about magic. Make all the characters human and the resulting story will be basically the same. It would change more by taking out the sex than by taking out the supernatural.

Or consider Joe Hill's *Horns*. Is it, technically speaking, fantasy? Is it horror? I will leave the answer to others – suffice to say that there is plenty of the supernatural. It is the story of a guy who grows a pair of horns, giving him psychic powers: a wonderful novel, which I have read twice. But it is not about magic, it is about a man searching for justice. Again, take the supernatural out of it, and the story wouldn't change all that much. The book does not ask how it feels to grow a pair of horns; the book asks how it feels to lose someone you love, and be unjustly accused of having killed them. It makes you think about evil. It does not make you wonder about the supernatural.

Look closely at most of the stories we classify as *fantasy* and you will find that the supernatural elements in them stand in for something else (I hesitate to use the words *metaphor* and *allegory*, because they are the refuge of bad writers who, being unable to tell a story, find the easy way out of preaching a gospel). The presence of these elements still speaks of something within us – there is a reason why I read the Southern Vampire Mysteries and not similar books with no vampires, and the reason is, the Southern Vampire Mysteries have vampires. But those elements are not what *makes* the story. The vast majority of romantasy books are indistinguishable from the previous breed of romances. They are not even less credible: the hunky cowboys and randy gentlemen which populated the translated Harlequin books my great-aunt used to read were not more 'realistic' than the werewolf and vampires of romantasy. Many grimdark books would have been Westerns if they had been written in a different age (and the smartest grimdark writers are perfectly aware of that).

I want to make it extremely clear that this is not a judgement of value. I picked *Horns* as an example exactly because it is a book I love. The best writers (and Joe Hill is one of them) know how to play with ideas. The main character in *Horns* becomes devil-like, and everybody believes he is some kind of devil, yet he is not – though he is not an angel, either. It is an interesting journey to follow. The stench of out-and-out metaphor is not there, and yet a reader can feel that what is on the page resonates with real-world concerns. All I am saying is that nothing there is inherently about magic. And *Horns* is only an example. Strange at it sounds, I would argue that most fantasy books have very little interest in magic.

Some do. And some books which have an interest in magic are not published as fantasy at all. My favourite example is Donna Tartt's *The Secret History*. Tartt plays the magical element so cleverly that, even though it is in plain sight, most people forget it is there. I will have to spoiler it gently, but not in a way which will ruin the reading experience, I hope.

The main characters are rich kids in an Ivy League university, except for one, an outcast on a bursary. Charmed by a teacher of classics, the group decides to work an ecstatic ritual to Dionysus, the Greek god of wine and frenzy. The ritual works – in the sense that the things which happen are the things that one who is working an ecstatic ritual to Dionysus should expect to happen. The book explores the fallout of that. You could not swap the ritual with anything else: if the characters did what they did after dropping LSD in a club, this would be a completely different story, articulating different themes and asking different questions.

On the full-fantasy end of the spectrum, Susanna Clarke's *Jonathan Strange and Mr Norrell* (one of my favourite books, for what it matters) is all about magic. A fascination for the idea of magic, and the human thirst for it, takes pride of place. The friendship and then rivalry between the two titular characters is not only coloured by magic, it is informed by it: if they were, say, sporting rivals, the book would be philosophically different. How does a magical mindset feel? What would it be like to live in a version of the nineteenth century where magic was as common as it was in historical Mesopotamia? These are some of the questions the book asks. Clarke has never stopped exploring the theme: her next novel, *Piranesi*, is a foray into magical thinking, playfully disassembling modern notions of space and time.

So, we have two different ways of writing magic. One, the most common, uses magic to colour the story. The colouring might be brilliant – but change it, and not much else changes. The second, which is more rare, uses magic to *draw* the story: you cannot touch the magical elements without changing the shape of the whole thing. In the first kind of book, magic is a feature. In the second, magic is a theme. The first kind of book is with magic, the second is *about* magic (though, of course, it can be about other things at the same time). Books of this kind are taking us back to an older mindset, the mindset of those who sculpted the Lion-man and painted the caves, of those who told the story of Gilgamesh. A mindset which knows that gods and spirits walk with us.

This is the kind of magic I have been chasing after, the elves I have been wanting to see. It is a quest which gives me random moments of joy, when I find the right story to read or write, but it can also be frustrating. Magic has a way of disappearing once you start explaining it: tight worldbuilding which clearly defines how magic works can be a lot of fun, and very cool, but does not feel *magical*. And yet, to casually throw strange elements into a story and refuse to tackle them at all is just lazy writing. Magic, when it is a theme rather than a feature, needs to *almost* – but not *quite* – make sense. It revels in ambiguity, doubt, indecision. It is impossible to understand, but beautiful.

Just like life, really.

You Do Not Need to Know How to Write a Book (Or How to Embrace Ignorance and Run with It)

RJ Barker

When it comes to writing books, I have no idea what I'm doing and once upon a time I played bass guitar. Those may seem like two decidedly unrelated clauses to you, but I promise you: as a sentence, it works. Or it will work by the time we get to the end of this, even though, right at this second, I am not sure quite how; just like I'm never sure how to write a book when I sit down to do it or how a book is going to play out until it has played out.

Don't tell anyone, though. This is just between me and you.

At the end of the book it all makes sense. It's all so obvious and I can clearly see exactly where I was going and what I was tilting at.

Of course it was about that.

Knew it from the start.

I'm a professional author and we're very clever like that.

I think there are experiences that are universal to writers. We talk a lot about not knowing what we're doing, imposter syndrome, fear of the page, feeling like we are simply not good enough to write this thing. It's the curse of any artistic endeavour[1] to never *know* if it's good enough. There is no definitive right or wrong. What one person loves with a rare and burning passion another may hate with its dark and seething twin. We are people who create something from nothing, and if you are at all familiar with physics, that's impossible. And yet we do it.

So if something goes against the laws of physics then that's magic, right?[2]

But, like all good magic, it comes with a price. You can't just go around making stuff from nothing, can you? No, of course not. And that lack of definition, the inability to *know*, is part of the price.

I'm not going to lie: writing is great, but I've never felt a rush like going on stage with a band in front of a crowd. The noise, the movement, the lights. There's very little that can touch that. At the same time, I have never felt as deeply wrong as I did when on stage with a band, I have never felt so powerfully and obviously out of place.

Art is complicated, I guess. But remember this bit for later, we'll circle back to it.

---

1   I'm steering away from the word 'creative' because every time I hear people refer to 'creatives' I want to do terrible things to them with a fountain pen.

2   I'm not a scientist. Don't email me about this.

Looking back, I know why I chased music (even if we remove the adolescent thrill of big hair and make-up being something forbidden and rebellious). It's because I saw myself on those stages: skinny boys who looked like girls and people who hadn't been to university. It didn't matter. The punk spirit and all that; you didn't have to be clever or to have passed your exams to do it.[3] So, for a kid who was desperate to create *something*, music made sense because, even though I loved books and was constantly reading, the truth of it as far as I knew was working-class kids from the suburbs of industrial Yorkshire towns didn't become writers. So yeah, becoming a rock star was a long shot, but writing and publishing a book?

I don't think that's happening, sonny Jim.

When you read this, if you read this, it will be nicely edited and it will flow and there'll probably be a theme and it will neatly tie up at the end. Writer magic, lies and more lies. If you saw this now, you would find paragraphs. Many paragraphs, and each one an unconnected thought that I am placing on the dreaded empty page while I search for whatever it is I am actually intending to say through the alchemy of the keyboard.

And it is alchemy, for me anyway.

Text to speech? No.

Handwriting? Never.

It is the act of typing that kicks into gear whatever it is in my head that makes words. I don't really understand it. I am often terrified of examining how or why it works in case what

---

3   Let's not talk about this, okay? Let's just say that maybe my earliest works of fiction were job applications.

I end up doing is performing an autopsy on my own golden goose. What use is it to me if I becoming aware of my artistic process ends with me poking at a corpse that will no longer squawk out anything useful.

Anyway, the bass guitar. I practised on that guitar. I made my fingers bleed playing it in a vain attempt to keep up with the people I was in bands with. The type of people who could hear a song once and play it right back to you, or tune an instrument while holding a conversation. For some people their instrument is a part of them, and when you are around those people you can feel it. Or I could feel it, and I knew I didn't have it.

You see, a bass player can wing it: hit the root note, stay on tempo, and you will be alright. I could actually do that. But at the same time that never felt creative, it felt like the least I could be doing, so I was always pushing, always working at the edges of my – well, *talent* is the wrong word, because I *worked* at it. *Ability*? Let's stick with that. I forced it and I still was barely able to keep up with those who just *got* it. The truth of it is, every time I picked up that instrument it felt uncomfortable in my hands, alien. It was heavy, the frets and the strings never just spoke to me the way they did to the people I played with.

But, and this is the weirdest part of it – I knew what I was doing. Or I knew what I should be doing. I learned the theory, what notes went where and how to click in with the drummer and provide counterpoint to the guitar and vocal. Knowing these things, well, it really just made it worse, because knowing a thing, I discovered, isn't the same as being able to do it.

What you might discover is how much you can't do.

I have pretty much convinced myself that no one knows how to write a book. (I suppose that is either a brave or a foolish thing to say in a book of essays about writing.) But yes, no one actually knows. I mean, we can write books about writing books, we can discuss character arcs or immerse ourselves in the hero's journey. We can world-build and we can plan and we can make charts, but every single one of those things is done for one purpose and one purpose only, and that is to give the writer the confidence to sit in the chair and write.

You'll hear lots of phrases used to describe different types of writers. Again, I remain deeply agnostic about these. Are you a planner or a gardener?[4] Do you make a meticulous skeleton and fill it in later or do you sit and write a book and see how it turns out?

Don't kid yourself, friend, these are both the same thing.

I sit and write a book and what I call my first draft is exactly the same process as someone who has sat and sketched out every chapter in their plan (although, admittedly, maybe it has more detail). Call me a 'gardener' if you want, merrily finding my way. But I would say that is me making my plan for the book. It's definitely not readable. I have to go through it again (and again and again and again) to know what I'm writing about and then make it actually work. Conversely, if you sit and do your meticulous plan, maybe that's just your way of gardening – a first draft to find out what you intend to do.

What does this have to do with no one knowing what they are doing? you may ask. Well, we like to give things names because

---

4   Or 'pantser', which I absolutely refuse to say as it's an ugly word.

that gives us a sense of control. We name our demon and that gives us power over it. But writing is not controlled, art in any form is wild and chaotic because at some point you have to sit down and make something exist that *has never existed in the world before*. You – *you!* – will create something only *you* can create. Set out a plan or fire it off from the hip, it makes no difference. At some point, you have to decide to conjure something from nothing, and no amount of anything will change the sheer *audacity* of that act. You will create people and places never seen before, and these people and places will feel real, and people you have never met and will never know will *care* about these people that do not exist.

Put like that it always sounds like a madness, and maybe it is. Ask a writer 'where do you get your ideas from' and maybe they'll pretend it's a bad question. It's not, it's a brilliant question. It's just a very hard one, because where do they come from? Where? Pointing at influences, at key moments that you can say 'oh, that came from that', is one thing. But entire novels? They are conjured from the ether, they are distilled from the alembic of life experience and imagination, and I am yet to meet a writer who can actually explain that moment of creation.

Because nobody really knows how to write a book.

* * *

Here's the thing about writing for me. And how we get back to the bass-playing thing and tie that in to the vague point I may or may not be making.

I do not know how to write a book.

But something happens when I sit at a keyboard and start to write. I become like those guitarists who could hear a song once and play it right back to you, or tune an instrument while holding a conversation. I am lost, but it simply makes sense, the words flow from my fingers (and it really does feel like that) and yeah, sometimes it's work and slog and writing things that I know I need to do to get me to the next place where I'm not sure what is going to happen, but I know I want to get there.

Then, I am lost again, words come, things happen and time passes and I am not aware of it. The laptop keyboard is my instrument, it never feels uncomfortable, or wrong, or difficult to use. It is always there waiting for me, and it very rarely lets me down. I never feel like I am working at writing – not that writing is not work sometimes, which sounds like splitting hairs, but if you know what I mean then you know.

If you don't then keep at it, and one day you will.

I don't want to give the impression, though, that a writer is some magical creature, floating through life in their own unique cloud being special and different to anyone else. Because we most assuredly are not. I might say it isn't work, but I must also stress it very much it is.

You are most likely reading this as someone who wants to be a writer, and as someone who is writing. Maybe you have realised that good ideas and the ability to get them on the page is not enough, there is something *more*. You are likely either in or heading towards a place of incredible difficulty. Because there comes a moment where you get good, but not good enough. It is frustrating, and this is the time when most of us start casting around for that 'one great trick' (TM poorly written internet articles) that will make it click, push you over the edge. The thing that will get the attention of an agent, or readers, or an editor, when the truth is there isn't one. You just have to keep on writing and shaving off those indefinable bits that are not quite right. Could I put my finger on them and tell you why? Probably not, because, as I've said, I do not know how to write a book. But I would know it wasn't right. I could give you pointers, but they would be for me and how I do things, and you are you. If I don't know how to write my book, then I definitely don't know how to write yours.

Did I mention I love it? Did I mention it makes me happy?

Now, you might think I'm saying you don't need to read books or essays about writing, or go to workshops or conventions and listen to people talking about how to write a book (which they probably don't know how to do). But you have to remember what I've been telling you all along. I don't know how to write a book. I don't know what it is that sets me off, I don't know why I feel so comfortable in front of a keyboard, I only know that I do. So, I don't know what it is that will set you off either. In the long run, writing is the only key that unlocks writing, but you never know what will give you the enthusiasm to *do the work*, or present you with a way of doing something that works *for you*. I have no idea how you will find that thing which will get you to sit down and write and finish something that gets you a step closer to being *there*, or lets you step into that moment when, for some reason I don't know how to explain, it suddenly becomes *right*.

I don't know when it happened, when I realised something and discovered the huge difference between wannabe musician me and writer me. It is not found in a book or on a course; it is something, like all magic, that is within me, and something that is within you.

I enjoy this.

I never enjoyed playing bass guitar. Oh, I wanted to do it, and being on stage was a massive buzz, but I never enjoyed the actual doing of it. For me, to write is to be enjoying myself, to create through the keyboard feels like where I should be. I jokingly refer to my ignorance in the title of this, none of us are ignorant because we are readers and every book provides us with a blueprint for how to write, it sinks into your brain. The fact is, if you read, you know how to write, the magic of it is only unlocking something you already have. Then honing it, planing off the rough edges until you have a voice that is uniquely you, a way of telling a story that could not be told by anyone else.

Like some neophyte magician in a classic fantasy book, you are setting out on a long hard road and there is no guarantee you will ever reach your destination, but don't let that put you off. There is never any guarantee we will reach *any* destination, and the only way to fail is not to try. So travel the road, knowing each step takes you closer to your goal, and enjoy it. There's no surer way to demoralise yourself and lose the magic of what you're doing than staring ahead at a destination that may seem very, very far away while missing the joy in where you are. Oh, and we're back to the bass guitar again. You see,

I never really wanted to be a musician. I wanted to be a rock star. It was not about the act of *doing*, never about that. It was about what I wanted to be. Writing is different: the doing of it is the fascination for me, the magic is in the act of sitting and writing. I'm not excited by receiving boxes of books, I really enjoy getting out and meeting people but I could live without it. It is the act of writing that brings me great joy, and as such, though I've been frustrated by the process, I've always been able to retreat to the act of just doing. Just writing. In that moment, whether I know what I'm doing and if I know how to write a book – well, that ceases to matter.

So maybe keep that in mind when you're frustrated, or annoyed with the entire process of it. No one really knows how to do what you are going to do, so try and enjoy the doing of it.

It occurred to me, as I was writing this, how terribly privileged I must sound – the published author going, 'Write cos you love it' – and let's not lie about this, I am lucky to be in the position I am in. Probably even luckier than you know. I'm too ill to do anything else, there was never and still is no plan B, and writing is precarious. Outside of being someone like George R.R. Martin, you're only as good as your last book. I can still remember counting every penny and wondering why I was even bothering because the goal seemed *so far away*. But then I would write and forget all else and I think that is the magic for me. The way that creating can grip you, can be a comfort and solace. In the end, I do not need to know how to write a book. Maybe you do not need to know how to write a book either.

You only need to be writing a book.

To make art of any type is to leap into the ocean, and the truth of it is you are the only person who knows if you are a strong enough swimmer to make it to the shore. Or, as we writing professionals call it:

'The End'.

Authenticity and Voice: A Reflection on What Voice Can Tell Us About Ourselves

Kritika H. Rao

If you're here, reading this essay, I am going to take for granted that you're interested in the craft of writing just like I am. Perhaps you're a new writer, seeking to understand the mechanics of writing. Or maybe you're a seasoned author, hoping for a deep dive into some techniques.

I find that no matter where I am in my career, I think of myself as both a new writer and one who is seasoned. I've been writing for as long as I can remember, but with each work there is an opportunity to grow and reinvent myself, while staying authentic to the stories and ideas that make my writing uniquely my own.

I almost always think of the act of writing as a surrendering to the ocean of ideas to discover hidden treasure. There are good days and bad days. On the bad days, each word is a whiplashing wave. No matter how much I wish to surrender, the wave fights back, leaving me tired and gasping on the surface. On the good days, I am submerged underwater, taken by the writing itself. I enter the zone, and tap into a whole different part of myself – an authentic self I find only with the tools of language, presented on the page just so. I speak to a lot of writers who feel similarly, and when we try to deconstruct what that 'zone' is, it's hard to quantify. It's the flow-state that athletes tap into, an almost ethereal state of being where you are so deeply entrenched into your words, so fully excavating the heart of what you want to say, that everything else disappears. It is this place that is the home of the authentic creative self, and one where I believe true voice lives.

They say you should write what you know. I think you write to *get* to know yourself. In a way, writing is merely an attempt to hold up a mirror to our minds, to peel back the masks and facades we live with and often try to convince ourselves of. For those few moments when it's just you and the act of expressing yourself, then writing is a kind of meditation. Before you show your work to someone else, presenting it to them for their judgement, writing is a quiet, rabid, *exciting* dialogue with yourself.

To be clear, I don't mean that the story tells you that you are this character or that, or that you would make this ethical decision or the other if you were in a character's place. Nothing as pedestrian at that.

I mean that in that act of contemplation when you're hunting for a word, when you're trying to decode a structure, when you *know* something is not working, all of those are acts of communion with your deeper self, your creative self. Each of those little hunts helps to hone your voice of instinct. Each of those builds trust with yourself. For a career artist, it is a lifelong endeavour – which is why I often feel like I am both new and practised in the art of writing.

From all of this, you might take away that as long as you enter the zone of authenticity, as long as you can submerge yourself into this ocean of ideas, the voice that you speak with – that creative voice – is going to be sublime, connected as it is to your realest self. That your work is going to come out sparkling, without any need for edits – perfect and precise, from the first step.

Quite the contrary.

Early in my career as a writer, I hit this zone several times; but looking back at my work, I can see that though there is authenticity, the voice itself was jagged. The treasure that I found, though still treasure, was of the surface variety, easily glimpsed from the shallows. I imagine years from now, when I look back upon the work I currently do, I will feel the same – for my own sight will have become clearer. I think it is a mistake to think of voice and authenticity as static selves. It's only when we learn to think of them as moving, shifting, evolving pieces of ourselves and our work that we can attempt to capture them at all. It is only when we continue to master our skill at diving – and remaining submerged in the ocean of ideas, coming up for air briefly – that we can find true treasure.

What is Voice?

Crack open any craft book and amidst different takes on plot, perspective, genre, dialogue, etc, another concept will lay itself bare on those pages, demanding to be examined. Voice. The word will peek out at you from every agent's and editor's wish list (*Above all, I seek a fresh and unique voice!*). Reviews will reference it, often to compliment an author (*A voice to watch!*), and sometimes to criticise them (*The voice was tired*). Yet when you sit down to examine what voice really is, it will skate away, cackling, leaving you bemused.

So what *is* voice?

Is it simply the way one writes? Is it a writer's style? Their choice of words? Their prose? Is it as simple as the manner in which a writer constructs sentences? The rhythm and cadence and musicality of one's work, or the themes that a writer returns to all the time – that, if you were to pick up any of their work, you would see shades of the same colour?

Or is voice more abstract than that, something so hard to pin down that one is reduced to simply saying, unhelpfully yet accurately, *I know it when I see it.*

I am a deconstructionist – and although I understand that trying to capture the essence of voice is a futile endeavour in some ways, I attempt it relentlessly. Especially for authors and works I admire, I like to get behind the final words on the paper. I like to take the story apart piece by piece and examine each part under a luminous lens. I question nearly everything, studying the work through light and mood. How did the author pull off this effect in this structure? How did they maintain such deep emotion with their character while presenting so much world-building information? What is it about their prose that makes stars dance behind my eyes? How do these sentences seize my breath in this way? How does the entire piece have such astounding rhythm that sounds leap in my ears, each word creating its own symphony? What is it about this work that *enchants*?

A lot of times, I can pull aside the veil. Structure, point-of-view, dialogue, even styles of prose can be taught and understood and examined piece by piece. I love finding the mechanics of a certain work, and seeing how those parts make the whole, and there is a lot of information to be gleaned from such an exercise. Yet I've realised the more I try to grasp voice, and reduce it into parts, the more it escapes.

By its very nature, voice is intangible. Voice is mysterious. Voice is complex to define, yet simple to detect, permeating a work so deeply that if you were to try and dissect it, you would see shadows and shades, but you would not be able to hold it – or at least, not do so very successfully and completely. I find I am not alone in thinking of voice in this manner.

Sunyi Dean, bestselling author of *The Book Eaters*, had a similar take on the concept of voice. 'Author voice to me,' she says, 'is an umbrella term for a complex combination of style choice, personality, influences, and unique perspective among other things. Controversially, that unique perspective isn't something you can teach.'

When I think of my favourite books, I can never quite remember what those books were fully about. I can recall elements of plot and structure, inventive and unique world-building, even the mood I was left with – joyful, cathartic, heartbroken. Yet, if asked, those parts would hardly make a coherent sentence, let alone pitch. I would not be able to tell you precisely why the book affected me in a profound way, but I will most definitely still pick up those books and read them again, and push them into your hands, because I will have retained a memory of *voice*. I will remember that this book made me sit up and take notice. This book left an imprint. This book *echoed* – and it was its voice that echoed, ringing through time and memory.

Prashanth Srivastava, bestselling author of *The Spice Gate*, agrees. 'Voice is something I remember books by, aside from just the plot or the character,' he says. 'It's likely a mixture of my brain simultaneously and subconsciously comparing it to other works of other authors I've read.'

When I think of voice in my own writing, I imagine it as the keenest, most soulful and vulnerable part of me that manifests itself in my work, almost without my permission and say-so. It is something that uniquely makes my work my own. You've all heard of it: the thought experiment where a hundred other people could take the same idea, choose the same perspective to write in (say, close limited third-person narrative). They could take the same plot elements, and structure, and character sketches, and they could plan out the story exactly as you would, saying this twist in the story occurs here, and this revelation occurs there. Yet they would not write the story in the same way you would. Prose, and the choice and arrangement of words, and other mechanical elements, are tools, of course – but the largest thing that would separate one author from the other is that invisible voice.

And in this age of AI writing, there is comfort to take from that. Nothing else will sound quite like your own work.

A Unique Perspective: We are not Our Work. But We Are.

Writing of any kind is a hermeneutic act – an invitation for the reader to enter a middle space with the writer, where the writer presents an idea and the reader witnesses it, and meaning is constructed between the two things. It is a halfway point of interpretation, a hand extended in offering, and another in receiving, where both the reader and writer collide, changing and evolving. And beyond the mechanics and the journey of the story, I find myself thinking it is this *voice* that transfers to the reader, forming the emotional core of the journey. Forming that bond of communication which is specific to the author *and* to the reader.

It is no wonder that reading, like writing, is so subjective.

If we are to agree that every writer has their own unique perspective that would make their story different to someone else's, all tools and mechanics remaining the same – then we can clearly chart a path to how each reading is different, too.

We can all crack open the same book, read the same story, but the way we interpret the story will be just slightly different than the person next to us – because we bring intangible sets of meaning that we ascribe to certain words. We bring our own biases and emotional resonance to each work, changed by the experiences of our lives that have led us to a point where we're encountering a work – until that work, in turn, changes us in some way as well. And so we move through life, encounter to encounter, transformed in some subtle way, and carrying that lexicon of meaning with us to guide our interpretation.

That is where the role of the reader comes in – but let's not forget that every author is their own first reader. In the very act of creation, there is information that the writer sees about themselves. Sometimes a writer will surprise their own self, able to chart the course of their own evolution through the work they create. Reading and writing are in many ways simply two sides of the same coin.

Consider, then, the writer as both the creator of the material and the audience for it.

I think of my epic science fantasy trilogy, The Rages Trilogy, starting with *The Surviving Sky*. In some ways, the trilogy is almost entirely a manifesto/fever dream of *how does magic work*, while deeply engaging with the idea of what humanity can mean. Even *The Legend of Meneka*, my Hindu mythology romantasy, is about a celestial dancer, Meneka, who questions through the book how to make an elusive magic her own, while battling themes of self-discovery. As is obvious through this essay, I enjoy deconstructing the ephemeral to understand how the world works, to seek patterns and closure as a way to process life. These themes almost inevitably make themselves apparent in my work, in large or small ways. What we observe of the world forms the core issues of our stories. It might not make itself apparent in theme all the time, but hidden between other elements of a story – between structure, dialogue, word choices and character motivations – our stories will inevitably hold up a mirror to the world we, as artists, see. And each artist's worldview will be just so slightly different.

Roshani Chokshi, bestselling author of *The Last Tale of the Flower Bride*, extends this into what we pay attention to. 'Specificity comes from what we, as artists, notice,' she says. 'And I think what links my work is I tend to notice the same things. In that I anthropomorphize whatever I can.'

So then, are we to conclude that we are what we write? I think that is reductive. Consider again the analogy of writing being akin to diving into an ocean of ideas to look for treasure. The treasure you seek is not the prose, the style, the point of view, or plot decisions. The treasure you seek is to be connected to that deep flow-state, to be submerged, where *voice* surrounds you. That *voice,* a thing that comes into existence based off your influences, your perspective, your ever-evolving personality, is a look into yourself. You are not what you write. But the more you dive, the longer you practise, the more you will inhabit your work in a way that only you can. You will leave an echo of yourself in your work with the unique voice that only you own.

If consuming literature is a hermeneutic act, then it is *voice* that forms the connecting tissue between writing and reading; voice, which truly conveys meaning in its subtle form. All language conveys meaning, of course, and narrative as a sum total is an instrument of meaning. But it is voice – personal, particular, profound – that carries the element of individuality.

It speaks – in layman's terms – from the heart of the writer to that of the reader. Books are like snapshots into an author's life. Authors are not their characters, or their worlds or stories. But we put so much of ourselves in our work. We mine our own hope, curiosity, intellect, culture and trauma, and we create fiction with that. We are not our books, but we leave something of ourselves in our books.

Is Voice Necessary? aka Can You Escape Your Voice?

Think of your favourite author. Your auto-buy author, whose every book lines your bookshelf. What is it about their work that you respond to? Think of your own work. Do you find yourself returning to the same themes and ideas, wanting to examine those in different ways and through different lenses? What does that tell you about your own viewpoint on life – your hopes, your sorrows, your judgements?

Every author has a unique voice. But that is not to say that every author is necessarily *voicy*. While I would argue that voice is one of the most important elements to make up a story, I would also hasten to add that voice is *one* of the many things to make a story, not the only thing. Each author chooses to employ voice differently.

Some authors spin a great yarn, without particularly worrying about leaving behind a particular voice. Others rely on voice to carve out their own authentic space. Most times, voice is *left* behind, as that elusive thing that is greater than its parts and comes into being because of writing. Very rarely, and most rewardingly in my opinion, voice *matures*, showing the writer's own evolution – developing almost without volition as the author continues to practise their craft.

From a beginner writer to a career one who practises the craft constantly, voice becomes clearer – at first, perhaps, being something that the author does not care much about, then slowly growing into a thing the author instinctively recognises in their own work. Voice, then, becomes a gut instinct – the feeling of looking at a piece of work and knowing whether it is right, whether something is missing, whether the words are landing in quite the right way. Plot, character, story decisions aside, a lot of times when a career writer is perplexed by their own work where something isn't quite *feeling* right, it can be a matter of voice – of nailing, or not nailing, something just so. As Rowenna Miller, author of *The Fairy Bargains of Prospect Hill*, says, 'All humans who write anything have a voice. That voice can be curated and refined and become an asset.'

I believe you never have to become a specifically *voicy* author. But it is a beneficial exercise to attempt to *understand* your voice, one way or another.

Publishing is a hard business, and baked into it is negotiation. Even editing is often a negotiation between you and your editor. Newer writers sometimes worry that they must listen to and approve every piece of feedback received from their editors, which is a slippery slope into losing your authenticity.

An editor's task is to help make the work the best version of what the *author* wants it to be. A good editor will almost never impose their vision on the work, but will in fact seek to help the author uncover their own vision, chipping away at the stone to help reveal the statue, not by sculpting it themselves, but by giving the author the right tools for the right shape.

An author unconfident in their voice is likely to take a hammer to the rock, destroying the statue even if the editor has only handed them the hammer to tap at one piece. An unconfident author might find it harder to parse feedback, seeing it only as criticism instead of an opportunity to examine and re-examine the work from different angles, and finally making a decision – even if the decision is not to change a thing. Having a good handle on your voice can help your negotiation with your editor – or with your beta-reader, reviewer, or critique partner. A good handle on voice helps establish confidence. As an authentic writer, you don't have to approve every piece of feedback that comes your way, but you should have the strength to *respond* to it, to examine it and see whether it makes your story stronger and your voice clearer – and then treat with it in such a manner. Voice is about trusting yourself. It is about trusting the journey you are on as an artist. And *that*, I would argue, is often a journey of self-discovery.

Voice as a Fantasy Author

Voice permeates genre, but in some ways it has particular importance for an author of fantasy fiction. Walk into a bookstore with a sizable fantasy section, and take a quick look at the works on the shelves. How many stories about dragons do you see? How many about fae? Demons, gods, mortals, lovers, heists, empires, the list of tropes is endless – as are the many stories that exist, containing these elements.

If you are a writer hoping to publish a fantasy book, you might be daunted by the idea of how to make your story original and fresh, while still being familiar enough that fans of one kind of book will make their way to yours. A hundred dragon books exist – those which are already published, and those which languish in an agent's or editor's inbox. Traditional publishing is far from a meritocracy – great books get overlooked all the time for a variety of reasons. But originality is one of the big ones that literary agents will often cite as a reason to reject manuscripts.

It is your voice that will make your work stand out from the slush pile. Human beings are creatures of pattern and familiarity, and readers often reward writers with loyalty, when we can make them look at the same thing they've been staring at slightly differently. Voice is one of those factors that does so most authentically.

Beginner writers often worry about writing to an exact readership, but no work will ever find as perfect a reader as the author themselves. If you are able to write something that you truly love – that you can read over and over again (because you'll have to during editing!) and still retain some measure of passion for it – then you've already achieved a kind of success. You are your first reader, and speaking with authenticity and allowing your work to do so will translate into a wider readership as well – with those who will respond to the cadence of your voice, even if the story you tell them is about yet another farm boy finding greatness as an unlikely king.

Evolving a voice as a fantasy writer has other benefits, too. A career author almost always experiments with genre and structure. You might start writing a piece of fantasy fiction today, which might follow familiar genre lines – but tomorrow, you might wish to reinvent the genre in strange, specific shapes, speaking to disparate things that only you uniquely make sense of. Consider the unique and wonderful voice of Martha Wells, whose many works are so different from each other, but who is very clearly the author of those works. The Murderbot Diaries have a very specific narrator voice to them, which is different from her Witch King series, which is different from The Raksura Series. Yet through all those, Wells's voice permeates – giving us a glimpse of the author. Those books are unmistakably hers, even though some are pure science fiction, others science fantasy, and still others fantasy.

Roshani Chokshi is another incredible example of this – whether writing for older audiences or younger, Chokshi's work has a specific rhythm, with stunning word play and vivid atmospheres, even though the books serve different audiences. Through these narratorial choices, the *voice* is clearly Chokshi's, so instantly recognisable that her Aru Shah books, and *The Last Tale of the Flower Bride*, and *The Gilded Wolves*, would sit well next to each other in a bookstore, if a bookstore were sorted according to *voice*.

Evolution of Voice

Earlier, I asked you to think about your favourite authors and what commonality you saw in their works, beyond themes and structures. I asked you to explore what you might have noticed in your own work, from years past and more current. Many writers choose to practise only in certain corners of the genre. Some others experiment beyond it or extend within it. Either way, for most writers who hone their craft consistently, you will notice their authorial voice maturing from their earlier works into their later works.

Charting this can offer insight into the evolution of an artist, where the voice becomes clearer and more confident with every telling. In fact, some might say that voice does not even become apparent until many hours of work have been put in. As Gabriela Romero Lacruz, bestselling author of *The Sun and the Void*, says, 'An author's voice is for me like an artist's art style. It can only be found with thousands and thousands of words written.'

Authors who work in the business for a while – and those who spend conscious hours cultivating their craft – will inevitably develop a sense for capturing their voice. Readers might respond to it in different ways, some citing tighter prose, vivid worldbuilding, or comparing an author's early work to a later one, with respect to style. But style, structure, plot, prose – all of these will differ from story to story. Most readers stick around because they enjoy an author's voice.

I think developing this voice consistently is one of the most remarkable journeys a writer can take when attempting to hold up a mirror to themselves and to the world. It is in some ways a huge privilege – for why do we write, if not to be heard or seen, even if it is only by ourselves? Voice, then, becomes more substantial. The pursuit of its discovery is the reason why many writers write at all.

SPOTLIGHT ON...
J.R.R. TOLKIEN

What Can Tolkien's Creative Process Teach a Writer Today?

Juliet E. McKenna

Reading *The Lord of the Rings* is a transformative experience for many would-be authors. Inspired, they put pen to paper or fingers to keyboard. As a result, especially since the 1960s mass-market paperback editions, publishers have received, and sometimes put into print, books which Ursula K. Le Guin described as 'commodified fantasy'. In her Foreword to *Tales from Earthsea*, reflecting on fantasy and science fiction in 2001, she was unimpressed by writing which:

takes no risks: it invents nothing, but imitates and triv-
ializes. It proceeds by depriving the old stories of their
intellectual and ethical complexity, turning their action
to violence, their actors to dolls, and their truth-telling
to sentimental platitude. Heroes brandish their swords,
lasers, wands, as mechanically as combine harvesters,
reaping profits. Profoundly disturbing moral choices are
sanitized, made cute, made safe.

In short, writing inspired by Tolkien all too frequently
resembles my first, never-to-be-published fantasy book. This
was memorably returned by one agent with the note: 'There's
nothing to distinguish this from the six other competent fantasy
novels which have crossed my desk this week.' That said, while
I believe taking *The Lord of the Rings* as a template is arguably
the biggest mistake a would-be writer can make, I find looking
at Tolkien's creative process does offer useful guidance. After
all, he must have been doing something right, for his work to
endure seventy years since its first publication in 1954/55.

The Shadow of the Past

The first insights into his process which most people read are
in Tolkien's own Foreword to the 1965 Ballantine edition of
The Lord of the Rings. This is assuredly a good place to start. It
is also useful to remember this was written with the benefit of
hindsight by an old man. Reading about Tolkien's life from his
childhood onwards, as well as studying his own writing else-

where, fiction and non-fiction, illuminates what's written here, as well as resolving some apparent contradictions.

Tolkien states in the Foreword's first paragraph: 'I desired to do this for my own satisfaction'. This is essential. There is no point in writing a book you are not passionate about. Getting a novel accepted by an agent and/or editor has never been easy, and that's only the start of the process. The author's belief in their book, and commitment to see it through, remain key to convincing publishers, large or small, to take on a project.

Though, as Tolkien somewhat obliquely states, 'I wished first to complete and set in order the mythology and legends of the Elder Days, which had then been taking shape for some years.' He is talking about material later published as *The Silmarillion* and in the subsequent *Unfinished Tales*, and *The History of Middle-earth*. Stanley Unwin, who had published *The Hobbit* in 1937, resolutely rejected successive attempts by Tolkien to submit versions of *The Silmarillion* as the promised sequel. Unwin wanted more hobbits. Eventually, Tolkien was persuaded and Unwin has been emphatically proved right ever since. An author's passion must be balanced by willingness to listen to publishing professionals. They may not always be wholly correct, and the writer may not necessarily be happy when they are, but an author who refuses to accept advice from the business perspective will get nowhere. Publication is a collaborative process. In my experience, constructive discussion usually finds productive middle ground.

Tolkien describes his work as 'primarily linguistic in inspiration'. This highlights one of the biggest traps lurking for the would-be writer, awe-struck by Quenya, Sindarin and so on in *The Lord of the Rings*. As a schoolboy, Tolkien learned Latin, Greek, French and German, and encountered Welsh and what was then called Anglo-Saxon. He spent his academic career working with language. As a philologist, he studied the history and development of words from Old English through to medieval literature. Any author without this background will struggle to create a convincing language for their imaginary world. Far too many make the attempt, and the artificiality of the results undermines their work. Just because Tolkien did this, today's fantasy writers really don't have to.

That said, it's worth digging a little deeper here. Tolkien's academic work involved looking for connections between ancient European languages and devising plausible theories about the transmission of words and shifts in meaning. This requires using informed imagination to create a plausible scenario. Tolkien studied epic poems such as *Beowulf* and *Sir Gawain and the Green Knight*, as well as lesser-known and fragmentary works. He was the first translator for some of these, and for a few, his version remains the only one. Tales of upheavals and heroism, the trials of kingship, and the threat of monsters in a remote and dimly lit age fired his imagination. We find direct evidence of works which he studied throughout *The Lord of the Rings*. The death of Theoden closely resembles the death of Theodorid, King of the Goths, in the Battle of the Catalaunian Plains. Tolkien's portrayal of his elves owes a great deal to his translations of Pearl, and of Sir Orfeo.

What can today's writer take from this? Let your imagination explore the things which you find intriguing. For Tolkien, this was language. For many of us, it is history, whether that's political, social or some other facet. Other authors find their starting point in economics. There are endless options. Find inspiration in what fascinates you, whatever that might be. This is where you will find the passion that will excite other people about your book. This will give you the resources to answer questions going beyond the words on the page, to convince an agent or editor that this story has the hinterland to make you more than a one-trick pony. Returning to this foundation, to rediscover that impetus, will sustain you through the hard days and difficult patches of a writing career.

Many Meetings

The folklore of Northern Europe was integral to Tolkien's work. He studied the Finnish *Kalevala*, the *Prose Edda*, and a multitude of other sources. He saw reading what has gone before as an integral part of creating new literature. In his essay 'The Monsters and the Critics', he speaks of a tower built of old stones which had formerly belonged to a more ancient building. Tolkien imagines newcomers finding the tower and pushing it over to look for hidden carvings, to discover where those stones had come from. They do not realise the tower had been built to see the distant sea.

Hopeful writers of fantasy can find reading such material extremely useful. We see echoes of these sources in novels by authors who followed Tolkien in the developing fantasy genre of the 1960s and 1970s. Original books that offered a new perspective include Alan Garner's *The Weirdstone of Brisin-gamen*, Susan Cooper's *The Dark is Rising* sequence, and Lloyd Alexander's *The Chronicles of Prydain*. These are merely the first titles that come to mind.

In his essay 'On Fairy Stories', Tolkien argues for the merits and importance of folklore and myth. In his view, these stories deserve respect. Writers today should take this one important step further. As the world shrinks thanks to the Internet, we have access to folklore, legends and mythology from global sources. This includes stories told by indigenous people which are integral to their belief systems and philosophies. Writers today need to respect material which they have not themselves grown up with. We must be aware of the complicated issues around cultural appropriation. Not everything we might read is fair game for anyone who might like to use it.

Not everything Tolkien read was so high-brow. We know he enjoyed popular fiction, including fantasy written well before he turned over a blank exam paper and wrote 'In a hole in the ground there lived a hobbit'. *The Lord of the Rings* is such a dominant presence in the modern fantasy genre that we can overlook what came before. In 1914, as an undergraduate at Exeter College, Tolkien used the money from the Skeat Prize for English to buy, among other books, William Morris's *The House of the Wolfings*. He was familiar with the works of George MacDonald, author of *At the Back of the North Wind*, as well as with *Alice in Wonderland*. We know the Tolkien children had E. Nesbit's stories read to them; these books were gifts from C.S. Lewis. I have no idea if Tolkien read such stories as Hope

Mirrlee's *Lud-in-the-Mist* or the works of Lord Dunsany, but these are further titles which fantasy writers today can usefully read to learn more about the roots of the genre. Though I advise reading with a critical eye for what will and will not work for contemporary readers.

Reading which we didn't like can also inspire us. In a letter to W.H. Auden, Tolkien mentions his 'bitter disappointment and disgust' at the coming of Great Birnam Wood to Dunsinane in Shakespeare's *Macbeth*. Clearly an army carrying branches didn't impress him. We see Tolkien's riposte in the march of the Ents on Isengard, and the huorns' arrival at Helm's Deep. Dernhelm's revelation to the Lord of the Nazgul takes Macduff's rebuttal of the witch's assurance that 'none of woman born shall harm Macbeth', and does something equally if not more dramatic with that idea. Crucially, this and other inspirations are woven seamlessly into Tolkien's narrative. *The Lord of the Rings* is a new creation with its foundation resting on what has gone before. The reader need not be familiar with any of these precursors for Tolkien's story to work. He is not simply sticking narrative elements together in some unconvincing pastiche.

Three is Company

In the Foreword, Tolkien also addresses the inspiration which writers can find in their own lives. 'An author cannot of course remain wholly unaffected by his experience...' However, he goes on to say, 'but the ways in which a story-germ uses the soil of experience are extremely complex, and attempts to define the process are at best guesses from evidence that is inadequate and ambiguous.'

Since *The Lord of the Rings* was first published, a great deal of scholarship has been devoted to analysing the aspects of Tolkien's life which appear to contradict this. Clearly, he valued groups of close personal friends, from the Tea Club and Barrovian Society of his school days in Birmingham to the Inklings and other groups in Oxford. We see this reflected in the Fellowship. The devastation of warfare on the Western Front undoubtedly informs descriptions of despoiled Isengard and ash-choked, desolate Mordor. Tolkien writes so powerfully of loss and death because he knew these things at first hand. Many more examples can be found.

This tells today's writer that drawing on personal experience, however difficult, will add depth and substance to their writing. However, an author need not lay their soul bare for all to see. The reader need not know anything of Tolkien's personal history for *The Lord of the Rings* to make an impact. As with other influences, where he is drawing on personal experience, that serves the story first and foremost. Writing as therapy rarely succeeds. Commentators have observed that readers find Tolkien's writing least accessible when it reflects his personal struggles most clearly, notably in 'Leaf by Niggle' and *Smith of Wootton Major*.

The Road Goes Ever On and On

We know Tolkien found inspiration in maps and the landscape around him. This is most explicit in *Farmer Giles of Ham*, but looking at the geography of Oxfordshire, Berkshire and Buckinghamshire turns up elements used in *The Lord of the Rings*. Theoden's standard is a white horse on a green field. Oxford is a short drive from Uffington and the most famous horse carved into the chalk hillsides of the Ridgeway. This is within walking distance of Wayland's Smithy and other pre-historic barrows. On the drive there from Oxford, you'll pass signposts to Buckland. The Rollright Stones can be found on the Oxfordshire/Warwickshire border. In the Foreword, Tolkien refers to Sarehole Mill, close to his childhood home, as an inspiration for the mill in Hobbiton, though he doesn't name it. Writers will definitely benefit from getting their heads out of their books and looking at the physical environment around them for ideas and settings. Getting some fresh air and exercise is a good idea as well, especially if progress on a book has slowed.

Does this mean a fantasy novel has to have a map? Along with invented languages, this is one of the fascinations of *The Lord of the Rings*, especially for those of us who read the hard-cover editions from a library, with the wonderful map to unfold at the back. That certainly set a precedent, and publishers will frequently ask for a map when they accept a fantasy novel for publication. It's useful to have something more polished than the rough sketches I drew literally on the back of an envelope while I was writing *The Thief's Gamble*. Fortunately, my husband trained as a draughtsman and was able to produce something my publisher could use. But a map offers more than a reference so the writer can work out travel times, and the reader can keep track of who is where.

A map broadens the scope of a secondary world, setting the story within a wider framework of geography and history. The more solidly grounded events are in what can be read as 'reality', whether that's contemporary, historical or invented, the more convincing the story becomes. That makes it easier for readers to take that extra step into the truly fantastic. Though it is only in Diana Wynne Jones's *Tough Guide to Fantasyland* that 'you are going to have to visit every place on this Map, whether it is marked or not'. Middle-earth offers many places for the reader to explore in their own imagination. Similarly, the Prologue and the vast amount of material in the Appendices show Middle-earth before and after the story he is telling. For many readers, this is why *The Lord of the Rings* stays with them long after they closed the book.

A Journey in the Dark

Given the amount of background material we know Tolkien amassed, does this mean he was a writer who planned the route of his story in advance? Or did he discover where that journey would take him once he had set out on the path? In the Foreword, he says the Scouring of the Shire was part of the plot from the outset. He talks of the references in *The Hobbit* to Gondolin, to the Necromancer, and other elements from mythology and legends of the Elder Days which he had already invented, which 'revealed the Third Age and its culmination in the War of the Ring'. In the following paragraph, though, he says, 'I stood by Balin's tomb in Moria. There I halted for a long while', and 'as the beacons flared in Anrien and Theoden came to Harrowdale I stopped. Foresight had failed and there was no time for thought.'

A writer can take several things from this. Firstly, dividing authors into those who plan and those who don't is pointless. Tolkien was neither and both. Every writer's process is different. The key is learning what works for you. Far more usefully, the Foreword highlights the importance of persistence. Tolkien says, 'I forced myself to tackle the journey of Frodo to Mordor'. Writing a book is a lengthy process. Every author finds times when inspiration is lacking and work becomes a stubborn trudge. The only way out is through, as various writers have said in various ways. The only alternative is giving up.

Many Partings

Is there a point where a writer should give up? We know Tolkien wrote and never finished *The Lost Road*, and *The Notion Club Papers* in the 1930s. A sticking point seems to have been the obstinate presence of America in this world as he wrote about crossing the seas to the undying lands of the west in Middle-earth. I mentioned my first and never-to-be-published fantasy novel. Recognising that book had problems which no amount of rewriting would solve was an essential step in my writing career. Authors need to develop this skill.

The good news is writing can be reused. Tolkien's poem 'The Adventures of Tom Bombadil' was first printed in the *Oxford Magazine* in 1934. Frodo's song in the Prancing Pony reworks a piece Tolkien wrote in 1923. In this Internet era, writers must be prepared for previously published work to be identified, but that's not necessarily a problem. It's definitely worth keeping a copy of incomplete or unpublished pieces. Stories which have hit some insuperable obstacle or tailed off without a conclusion can be a source of fresh ideas when inspiration for a work in progress runs dry.

All That is Gold Does Not Glitter

Tolkien understood that a story must engage the reader on different levels. In his Foreword, he explains his motive for writing *The Lord of the Rings* as 'the desire of a tale teller to try his hand at a really long story that would hold the attention of readers, amuse them, delight them, and at times maybe excite them or deeply move them'. Let's consider how he strives to achieve these aims.

He knew that a story must be enjoyable. In 'The Monsters and the Critics', he argues for the merits of *Beowulf* first and foremost as a poem to be enjoyed, rather than criticised for its deficiencies as a historical source or judged against a different literary style. Writers such as W.H. Auden recall Tolkien as a younger man at Oxford in the 1920s and 1930s, holding undergraduates spellbound as 'he recited, and magnificently, a long passage of *Beowulf*'. A Canadian postgraduate wrote: 'He came in lightly and gracefully... his gown flowing, his fair hair shining, and he read *Beowulf* aloud... The terrors and dangers that he recounted – how I do not know – made our hair stand on end.' Michael Innes (J.I.M. Stewart) wrote: 'He could turn a lecture room into a mead hall in which he was the bard.'

Tolkien understood that a reader must find points of connection. *The Lord of the Rings* opens with the amusing and entertaining episode of the long-expected party, which centres the entire story on the hobbits. From the outset, readers can identify with these characters. Their lives most closely resemble our own, or at least, it's a life which we are familiar with thanks to books, movies and TV.

Hobbiton has comfortable homes, afternoon tea, birthday parties and fireworks. With jokes, such as the Gaffer grumbling 'I don't hold with wearing ironmongery, whether it wears well or no', Tolkien uses humour to strengthen the connection between the reader and the hobbits. He does this with care and precision, and it is worth noting the differences between the Shire as portrayed in *The Lord of the Rings* and in *The Hobbit*. It remains a bucolic, very English haven, with a postal service, inns and eating-houses, but we do not find amusing references to notes left under the clock on the mantelpiece and incongruous anachronisms like the contract terms offered to Bilbo by Thorin & Co. in *The Hobbit*.

The variations in Tolkien's prose style throughout *The Lord of the Rings* should not be overlooked. Writers can learn a great deal from studying his choices for different episodes in the narrative. The passages featuring the hobbits are presented in what literary criticism calls a 'low mimetic style', placing characters and readers on the same level.

Other characters from Aragorn to Boromir, Gimli and Legolas, to Eomer of Rohan, and Faramir in Osgiliath, are written in a more epic style, using 'high mimesis' in both description and dialogue to create a degree of distance between them and the reader. Figures like Gandalf, Galadriel and Sauron have still more elevated, mythic qualities, and this is reflected in the prose, making them more remote.

Today's writers should also note how prose styles have moved on since Tolkien's day. Influenced by cinema and television, fiction is more dialogue-driven and inclined to focus on individual points of view, whether from a third- or first-person perspective. Lengthy descriptive passages and the extended use of narrative summary look back to the Victorian and Edwardian fiction which Tolkien grew up reading. It's instructive to see how Tolkien's own approach as a writer developed. The narrator's voice with an omniscient viewpoint which is a feature of *The Hobbit* is absent in *The Lord of the Rings*.

Old That is Strong Does Not Wither

Entertainment and engagement are not enough. Tolkien says he wants to move readers deeply. On the other hand, he insists in the Foreword that: 'As for any inner meaning or "message", it has in the intention of the author none. It is neither allegorical nor topical.' But elsewhere, in a letter to a Jesuit friend in 1953, he says:

> *The Lord of the Rings* is of course a fundamentally and religious and Catholic work; unconsciously at first, but consciously in the revision. That is why I have not put in,

or have cut out, practically all references to anything like religion, to cults or practises, in the imaginary world. For the religious element is absorbed into the story and the symbolism.

How can we resolve these apparent contradictions in a way that offers writers today useful guidance?

Clearly, *The Lord of the Rings* is not an allegory. Comparison with acknowledged allegorical fiction such as C.S. Lewis's Narnia stories, and his science-fiction trilogy starting with *Perelandra*, makes this obvious. That hasn't stopped commentators trying to force *The Lord of the Rings* into a framework that fits what they want the story to be, but their convoluted arguments inevitably fall apart, whether they are trying to present Frodo or Aragorn as a Christ figure or something else. This is a factor in *The Lord of the Rings'* lasting appeal. Many readers find recognising the underlying Christian messages in C.S. Lewis's writing ends their enjoyment. *The Last Battle* is frequently cited as an example of an author setting out to send a message and ultimately delivering an unsatisfying read.

The War of the Ring is also not topical. In the Foreword, Tolkien shreds the theory that it's some thinly veiled analogy for the Second World War himself. Topicality inevitably dates a book, and the more obvious that is, the faster the story becomes irrelevant. *The Lord of the Rings* is a timeless narrative. Middle-earth exists outside our own world, with underlying themes of ongoing relevance to the human condition. This universality helps explain the book's enduring popularity.

So where does the Catholicism come in? In the Foreword, Tolkien says, 'its main theme was settled from the outset by the inevitable choice of the Ring as the link between it and *The Hobbit*'. Choices are central to the story. Frodo chooses to take the Ring to Mordor, though he does not know the way. His friends choose to go with him. Galadriel chooses to diminish and go into the west rather than become a queen as beautiful and terrible as the morning and the night. Boromir chooses to try and take the Ring. Faramir does not. Sam chooses to return it. Denethor chooses despair. I could go on, and on.

Despair is, of course, a mortal sin. The Catholic cardinal virtues underpin other critical choices and turning points in the plot. Prudence is the wisdom to assess an action and its likely consequences. Justice is centred on fairness. Courage is not macho sword-swinging, but endurance and the resolve to confront dangers despite being afraid. Restraint is self-control. We see these at work within the story, but virtues and vices are not the exclusive property of the Catholic Church. This ethical framework appears in writings by Plato, Cicero and others. Once again, the lack of specificity in Tolkien's writing enhances its applicability which he saw correctly 'resides in the freedom of the reader'.

Which is all very interesting, but what does this offer by way of creative writing advice? Well, Tolkien's writing is consistently true to his personal moral and ethical code. That's solid advice to follow, however your own beliefs and worldview might differ from his. This will give depth and substance to your writing, if you hope to offer more than transitory entertainment.

Journey to the Crossroads

In more practical terms, the centrality of personal choice in the story influences other story-telling decisions worth noting. Magic in *The Lord of the Rings* resides primarily in items such as Galadriel's mirror and the palantiri rather than in people. Magic items play their part at key moments, such as Sam's desperate need for a light in the darkness of Cirith Ungol, but enchantments do not of themselves resolve dangers or dilemmas. Individual characters must do that by choosing the right path. Writers should note how unsatisfying the story would become if magic cut through the moral and physical challenges the characters face.

Evil arises when the wrong path is taken. Isildur chose not to destroy the one ring when he cut it from Sauron's hand. Pride led the nine kings to accept the rings that turned them into wraiths. Smeagol murdered Deagol out of greed and became Gollum. Saruman chooses an alliance with power rather than resistance. This makes these threats far more menacing and relatable. The quest to destroy the Ring becomes much more than a trip to overthrow motiveless malignity.

Though we must also note that the nature of evil is not as clear as it might be, certainly to readers today. Writing decades ago, Tolkien made extensive use of the well-worn convention established in legend and epic that goodness is bright and beautiful while evil is dark-skinned and twisted. These days this is rightly problematic, notwithstanding Sam wondering whether or not an Oliphaunt rider was truly a bad man or not.

Writers today must consider which conventions from myth and folklore have outlived their usefulness. Where these have become actively offensive, it's time to take a different path.

There and Back Again

Tolkien made his choices and wrote his story. The Foreword tells us, 'when the "end" had at last been reached the whole story had to be revised, and indeed largely rewritten backwards'. This brings us to finding and handling feedback. Tolkien accepts that 'it is perhaps not possible in a long tale to please everybody at all points', and this is definitely something writers should bear in mind. That said, while Tolkien says 'as a guide I had only my own feelings', there is considerable evidence in his letters and papers that he made changes to *The Lord of the Rings*, undoubtedly to the benefit of the book. Fresh eyes will pick up what the author is too close to see.

Chapters were sent to his son Christopher, serving in South Africa during the Second World War. It's a matter of record that Tolkien read sections of the work in progress to his fellow Inklings, and listened as they shared what they were writing. Finding one close, trusted friend who can discuss a project in depth and in detail, and a wider circle more representative of the unknown reader who picks up the novel in a bookshop, is pretty much ideal. Though Tolkien didn't necessarily always think so. C.S. Lewis writes, with what reads like exasperation, that Tollers' response to criticism was to ignore it entirely or to rip up what he had written and start again. *Not* doing what Tolkien did is better advice here.

Revising a first draft – and however many subsequent drafts your individual process requires – is essential, and not just to correct spelling and punctuation. The big picture comes into focus and the underlying themes of a novel become apparent. The writer can decide how to use these to enhance the narrative. Loose ends make themselves known and the author can choose to tie them up – or not. It's worth noting the questions Tolkien leaves unanswered, such as the origins of the barrow wights or the background of the corsairs. Some readers are left unsatisfied. For others this adds to the sense of a wider world with a history before and after the War of the Ring.

The Last Debate

Revisions must come to an end. Learning when to let a book go seems to be something Tolkien never learned. These days neither readers nor publishers will patiently wait for seventeen years for a sequel to a successful first novel. It's also apparent that Tolkien was not very astute when dealing with the business side of publishing. In 1950, he began negotiations to leave his long-established publishers Allen & Unwin, in hopes that Milton Waldman of William Collins would put *The Silmarillion* into print. Stanley Unwin still steadfastly refused. Letters relating to this attempt do not show Tolkien in a good light. As it turned out, Waldman demanded extensive rewrites to *The Lord of the Rings*. When Tolkien wouldn't countenance this, Collins withdrew their offer. It's only thanks to Rayner Unwin, Stanley's son, that the book was finally published.

Even so, Tolkien continued to pay little attention to business concerns. The Foreword became necessary when Rayner Unwin and Tolkien's authorised American publisher, Houghton Mifflin, learned an unauthorised paperback edition of *The Lord of the Rings* was planned by Ace Books, taking advantage of a loophole in US copyright law. Tolkien was supposed to deliver the Foreword in time for the Ballantine Books paperback to be published first. This was another deadline he missed. A writer today must be far more organised and professional to sustain a writing career.

Though, to be fair, the seventeen-year delay between *The Hobbit* and *The Lord of the Rings* was not entirely down to Tolkien. The Second World War was a considerable distraction and interruption, to say the very least. Even without that, Tolkien could not work on his fiction full-time. *The Hobbit* was a success, but he was in his sixties before *The Lord of the Rings* brought in a substantial income, along with a hefty tax bill. He held academic posts at Leeds and Oxford Universities to support his family throughout his writing career. As he says in the Foreword, during the writing of *The Lord of the Rings*, 'I changed my house, my chair, and my college'. Once the book was complete, 'it had to be typed, and re typed: by me; the cost of professional typing by the ten fingered was beyond my means'.

So last, and by no means least, Tolkien's career should reassure today's writers that having a day job doesn't make them any less of an author.

Creation Magic

Worldbuilding is one of the fundamental aspects of fantasy fiction. From heroic epics to surreal visions of alternate dimensions, your story can succeed or fail on the strength of the world you have imagined. As much as the characters themselves, the environment they exist within will draw your readers in and intrigue them to keep turning the page – or maybe challenge them with its creativity and vision.

There are many questions to ask when starting to create a world. Is it based in known history, or is it an alternate universe, parallel to our own but different? What are the rules of this world? Who is in power, and where does their dominance spring from? Is there magic here? Are there monsters? What are their clothes made of, where does their food come from, what monetary system do they use…? It's easy to get lost down the rabbit hole.

These three essays look at the art of playing God from three perspectives, offering different ways through the maze of creation itself.

Building a World and Getting Away with It

Jen Williams

A good place to start with this sort of thing is to ask: what is fantasy? And why is it the greatest of all genres?

There are probably concise, academic answers, but I think when we ask 'what is fantasy?' it really all boils down to: This World is not our World. We're Not in Kansas Anymore. And if you want to get deep into secondary world territory, and you take magic to be an essential ingredient, then it's probably: This World Could Never be our World. For me, fantasy is about being transported, about going somewhere you've never been before, and a large part of the heavy lifting when it comes to writing this genre is making the reader believe wholeheartedly in it, even when every detail tells them this place could never exist. This world contains a lake of serpents that sing the future; in this world, every child born under a full moon can move objects with their mind; this kingdom sails through the clouds on the back of a vast beetle. Making your reader believe is an impressive magic trick, like whipping away their chair to leave them still sitting, suspended in space.

And as for the question of why fantasy is so great, well, fantasy is great because it lets us escape. All fiction is in some way transportive, of course, but in terms of escapism, fantasy is the genre that gives you a whole new world to disappear into. Escapism is treated like a dirty word, but I would argue it's vital. In our world, this climate-borked, war-torn, fragile little planet full of people making poor decisions, we need to be able to step away for a moment to a place that still contains a rainbow of possibilities. If you're constrained, oppressed, suffering, how can escape be bad? To escape to a better life is a deeply human urge, and the brilliant thing about humans is that we can manage this with our imaginations alone. And being able to dream of better worlds helps us to create them in the here and now. If you don't believe it from me, Ursula K. Le Guin herself once said, 'Fantasy is escapist, and that is its glory', in an essay where she was paraphrasing J.R.R. Tolkien, and you could hardly name two more important figures in the field than these giants.

It all got a bit serious there, didn't it? But I love fantasy, you see, and to talk about how you build it, I need you to know why it's important.

* * *

So, this world that you're building – how do you go about doing that?

What you want is for the reader to step into your story and trust that the flagstones will hold them up rather than drop them into the void, and that solidity is not easy to conjure. Any sane person presented with a city on the back of a vast flying beetle is going to have a lot of questions, such as: why don't the buildings slide off? How are people breathing up there? And how does the beetle feel about all this? You as the writer have to provide excellent answers to those questions, like: the beetle excretes a sticky residue that the citizens of Carapacia use to construct their buildings; over generations they have adapted to the thin atmosphere; she considers it her holy mission to safely shepherd the tiny humans of Carapacia through the turbulent storms. I would argue that coming up with these answers is where writing is at its most delicious, and certainly it's one of the biggest reasons that I love writing in this genre. Answer these questions well and your reader will be able to strut confidently across a tiny section of that giant iridescent wing-casing and think nothing of it. They certainly won't think about the remarkable magic trick you've just performed.

* * *

You are the creator. You are the god of this world, and like any god, you need to know how the moving parts work. The more detail you have fizzing around your brain, the better – or so the argument usually goes, and details are important, I won't argue with that. Playing around with details can often lead to some beautifully unexpected creations, some that might even become the bedrock of your story. Perhaps you create an order of priests whose sacred purpose is to collect the holy excretions of Volkasgäd the Sky Beetle, a perilous occupation which requires them to climb down between its vast glistening mandibles. And perhaps one day the youngest of them slips and spins on the rope, finding themselves staring into the glittering abyss of one gargantuan insectile eye, and they are gifted with a vision that changes the course of their life... Following these paths could lead anywhere. They could lead to the story you're supposed to write, for example.

The 'worldbuilding is king' approach to writing fantasy argues that you should have all these details in your head when you start writing, so when your abseiling priest pauses on some chitinous bump to have a spot of lunch, you know what is inside his pack when he opens it. You know, in fact, where he buys the small, hard, black apples that he eats with his cheese, and you know the fly-blown, guano-fed orchards where those nightmare apples are grown.

Which is all very well, but be wary. This is a trap. It's all too easy to get lost down these roads, gathering more and more detail to yourself like that creature in the rubbish tip in *Labyrinth* who insists to Sarah that *all* of these things are important, all of these things are *treasure*. You can end up with notebooks and brains groaning with detail when, actually, how much of it needs to be on the page? How interested really is the reader in the precise mixture of bat and bird droppings used to fertilise the nightmare trees? No, wait, that actually does sound interesting. But how much do we really care where the priest buys the cloth that she uses to sew the glittering cloak she wears over her robes? Is it vital that we understand precisely how many silver bits make a gold bob? Or how the sewers work? The key here is balance. Know what you need to know and where to use it. Easier said than done.

* * *

I often get asked about worldbuilding because the world at the centre of the Winnowing Flame trilogy is, I would say, reasonably complicated. In these books there is a world called Sarn which, every few generations, is invaded by an army of terrifying insectoid creatures called the Jure'lia who are intent on consuming every living thing. The only people who were ever able to repel these invaders were the Eborans, a race of long-lived, supernaturally elegant hyper beings, this world's answer to elves – a bit like Tolkien's, but not as warm and cuddly. The Eborans had a magical tree god that furnished them with war-beasts, creatures from myth that aided them in their battles against the Jure'lia. And then, in the last great war, the tree god was killed, and the Eborans lost their near-immortality and their war-beasts. To make matters worse, it was discovered that drinking human blood gave them a shadow of their former powers, and consequently relations with the human occupants of Sarn took a sharp downward turn... Obviously, this is already A Lot. I'm asking the reader to believe in elves, in an army of giant maggot ships and a terrifying hive mind queen. I'm asking them to believe that griffins and dragons and winged wolves can be birthed from the fruits of a giant tree.

And really, that's not even half of it. Sarn also has a sect of women able to drain the life force from any living thing and repurpose it as a green flame that can burn things a normal fire can't. The Winnowry has grown up around these women, an evangelical organisation dedicated to keeping them 'in their place', which, according to the Winnowry, is prison. And the world itself is poisoned and strange, with vast mutant creatures prowling the overgrown forests, and that's not to mention the parasite spirits, ephemeral beings of jelly and light that can turn you inside out if you happen to brush one of their fronds. Also, giant bats.

I wrote *The Ninth Rain* directly after finishing the Copper Cat trilogy, which was more directly in conversation with sword-and-sorcery fantasy and its tropes. The Copper Cat books were partly a love letter to a more traditional kind of fantasy, and consequently the world felt a lot more familiar. The place where famed mercenary and mead-drinker Wydrin of Crosshaven plied her trade was filled with taverns and dungeons and mysterious temples; the reader will know these streets a little already, because they have walked the alleyways of Lankhmar and Ankh-Morpork. With the trilogy that became the Winnowing Flame, I wanted to do something different. Namely, I wanted to create a new thing that was entirely my own.

(Quick caveat: there are no new things under the sun, in writing at least, and anyone who has peeked at this trilogy will see the fingerprints of other, greater stories all over it – Robin Hobb's Realm of the Elderlings, *Princess Mononoke*, Guy Gavriel Kay's *Under Heaven*... All writers are formed from a maelstrom of influences, and if you're lucky, sometimes something that feels shiny and new can happen.)

The real trick of all these things – the insect invasions, the tree god, the war-beasts, the elves, the giant bats, the winnow fire and the parasite spirits, all that jazz – is that they are all linked. One is born out of the other – you take one element out and the filigree constellation I've built doesn't quite work. People have asked me about it occasionally, and usually the assumption is that I had all this figured out in advance; that I had built this complicated framework in a notebook and dumped it wholesale onto the page, then slotted my characters in around it.

Which is not the case at all. In fact, most of it is reverse engineered.

* * *

This is the part where I say mildly controversial things about how worldbuilding traditionally works and how I personally use it.

For me, stories are about people. That's not the controversial bit. I actually think it's pretty undeniable. Everything, ultimately, from complex historical fiction about the Tudor court to an epic quest by a bunch of rabbits to find a new home; from a trio of ghosts in a graveyard spying on a grieving Abraham Lincoln to a very hungry caterpillar (no, really, we've all been hungry, right? We've all transformed ourselves at one point or another, right?) – all stories are, at their heart, about people. Or any stories worth their salt, anyway. Even very high-minded science fiction dealing with the nature of the universe is still viewing that universe through a human lens, even if that's by contrast. We're still present in there somewhere.

Stories are about people, so people are where I start.

When I was planning *The Ninth Rain*, I knew that I wanted to write about a scholar. It was a fantasy archetype I hadn't played with before, not really, and I usually like to try something different with each book. Initially I thought the character might be young, possibly even a young, ineffectual man (Presto from the old *Dungeons and Dragons* cartoon came to mind for some reason) but nothing particularly excited me about that. We've all seen that character before, right? There is something fun about watching an inexperienced little guy who is generally useless gradually come into their own over the course of a book, but it wasn't a story I felt compelled to write. When that didn't work, I started to think about the opposite. What if this character was experienced, knowledgeable, just brimming with gumption and confidence? What if she was older? Someone who had, perhaps, spent a great portion of her life being responsible for other people and was just now being given the chance to do what she wanted. It's curious, the alchemy of character creation. You can labour over it for hours, days, weeks, and eventually you might have someone you want to write about, if you're lucky. And sometimes, when the gods are smiling on you, a few stray thoughts can summon a character who steps fully formed into your head. Lady Vincenza 'Vintage' de Grazon was that sort of character. A blessing, in other words.

I knew then that she was a scholar, and more than that, she was a strong-willed independent woman with a will of steel and a kind heart. If she was a scholar – an extremely determined one – then I would have to give her something to study, something to investigate. Clearly this world would need a mystery to solve. I wanted to give Vintage the juiciest possible world to explore, because frankly she deserved it, and that meant a world full of weird and dangerous creatures no one quite understood. I knew that Vintage was what we might call a naturalist, or a student of natural history, and she'd want to know why her world was full of things that wanted to kill her.

There's a sequence in the science-fiction video game *Mass Effect 2* where you have to explore a vast, abandoned spaceship. It's a properly alien structure, and it's extremely eerie and quiet, so the tension rises as you turn each corner. Eventually, of course, terrible things come to light and you and your little team have to fight for your lives. The collector ship sequence is a standout scene in an exceptional story, and it stayed with me long after I had played the game to death. Wouldn't it be great, I thought, if Vintage could explore a ship like that? She would *love* it. And so, I put them into the story for her to poke around inside. From there, the nature of the Jure'lia grew, and that in turn changed the whole nature of *The Ninth Rain*. I originally conceived of it as your classic high fantasy adventure, but the addition of things that seemed to come from a place not of Sarn, well… the genre itself began to shift and change. And all of that led out of the question: what would be the most interesting world for Vintage to explore? It changed the book fundamentally.

* * *

We talk about the first draft a lot when we talk about writing books, partly because it is the biggest, most obvious mountain you have to climb. Anyone thinking about writing a novel has to face that vast edifice of words, so naturally it's the thing people want to know the most about. How do you start a first draft? How do you get it to hang together? And how do you wring one hundred thousand words out of your brain?

This is all valid, but we should talk about the second draft more than we do, because it's an incredibly useful tool and, in my opinion, integral to the building of worlds. When I decided, about thirty thousand words into the writing of *The Ninth Rain*, that I wanted Vintage to explore a crashed alien ship, that changed the bones of the book. I'd already written a hefty chunk of it; that first thirty thousand didn't include anything about the Jure'lia being potentially otherworldly. And as I continued writing the first draft, more things grew out of the demands of the characters. I wanted Tormalin and Hestillion to be two of the last Eborans in Ebora, because I wanted their situation to be desperate – if they were desperate, they might do unwise things (you always want your characters to be doing unwise things – if everyone is deeply sensible, you have nothing to write about). So, to isolate them both, I created a disease from the drinking of human blood that wiped out much of the Eboran population. As for the fell-witch Noon, the young woman able to summon an eerie emerald flame from her hands, I had to give her a source for those powers and… well, some things are too much of a spoiler for an essay, I suppose.

By the time you get to the end of the first draft, a lot of things have changed. It may even be that the book bears very little resemblance to the novel you planned at the very beginning (if you're me, at least). This is where the second draft comes in. Here, you can make it look like you had all that stuff in mind from the very start. Writers all have very different feelings about editing, and the second draft is a kind of edit. Personally, I find it to be one of the most rewarding stages of the book, the place where you can expand on everything you've seeded in the first draft, pulling out themes and weaving together disparate strands of story so they come together into something you only glimpsed a part of when you were planning it.

The second draft is especially important for fantasy writing and worldbuilding. By the end of the first draft, you'll have a much stronger idea of your world – your characters have helped you build it, after all – and here you can strengthen and refine it. Which is another reason why, in my opinion, you don't need to have all this figured out before you create that Word document (other writing programs are available). If anything, leaving space for the world to grow organically as you write is vital. Even the characters I've started the journey with have usually changed in the course of the book, and one of the great satisfactions of the second draft is sharpening them up into their true selves. The earliest sketches of Tormalin the Oathless were of an essentially heroic, angsty man with excellent hair. It was only with the exploration and discovery of the first draft that I found him to be vain, arrogant, kind-hearted and fastidious; all aspects of his personality I enjoyed bringing out in the second draft. The exception here was Vintage. She was such a strong presence from the start that she changed very little from first to second draft, although I discovered plenty about her as I went along: her fondness for her nephew, her investment in Sarn's prototype steam railway, plus a past romantic liaison that would have a big impact on the overall story.

* * *

You start with a character, and then you create the world that gives them the most (interesting) trouble. It *does* need to be interesting trouble. It can't be, oh, this person is bad at maths and in this world they have to do a self-assessment tax return – that's not interesting, that's just my life.

Let's say you want to write a story about a young woman who is consumed with wanderlust. She's led a sheltered life, dreaming of the world beyond her doorstep, and finally circumstances have arranged themselves so that she can leave home. Give her a world that's wondrous, dangerous, or downright difficult to explore. Maybe she has lived her whole life on the back of a vast beetle, and no one knows for sure what waits beyond the clouds that circle the teeming city of Carapacia.

Or let's say you want to write about a young man who has a sharp, curious mind and a sharp, lethal sword. He's heard stories all his life about giant beasts in the sky, but in the tiny valley where he lives, the sky is always obscured by clouds. Only by scaling the highest mountain can he catch a glimpse of the world-beetle, the myth he has been hunting all his life...

If you're reading this, I've assumed you have some interest in writing fantasy (if you don't, and you've just ploughed through the last three thousand words – oh god, I'm so sorry). Maybe you've written a number of fantasy novels already, or you're at the beginning of your journey. If the latter is the case, then I want you to picture yourself as the protagonist. You have a great haircut, a fancy cloak and a go-get-'em attitude. You've filled your pack with bread and hard cheese, maybe a bottle of your uncle's best mead, and you're wearing the mysterious medallion that you found in the wood under the full moon, the medallion that sings in your dreams about the path that leads away from town. You have a little bit of room left in your pack, so you decide to visit the witch that lives by the twisted old hornbeam tree, to see if she has any wisdom to pass on before you set off, or, failing that, any sausage rolls she's willing to part with.

She hands you an old leather-bound book. On the inside, written across the yellowed pages in faded purple ink, are the following pieces of wisdom:

Fantasy is the greatest genre because it lets us escape.

To believe in your story, the reader must believe in your world.

You need to know your world.

You probably don't need to know where your potatoes came from. Unless the potatoes are very important to your character.

Stories are about people.

Ask yourself who you want to write about, and then create the world around them.

Let your characters and your story grow organically, and follow where they lead.

Use the second draft to make yourself look like a goddamn genius.

Above all, take all writing advice with a healthy pinch of salt, even – or especially – when it comes from your friendly local witch. Ultimately everyone finds their own path, and the only way to do that is to get out there and start your own journey. Throw everything at the wall and see what sticks. Get lost in the creation of your own world, or fall in love with your characters and let them show you it. All I can tell you is what works for me, and what I've learned while sitting at my desk, following the paths that lead over the horizon.

You shove the journal inside your pack, check one last time that the witch definitely doesn't have any sausage rolls – they'd be more use than this book, probably – and you turn from her door, ducking under the low-hanging branches of the hornbeam, and then you're on your way, down the path and over the hill. Good luck.

Brick by Brick,
Word by Word

Jeff Noon

I imagine that many writers start with a story they want to tell, and then build a world around that story, a suitable location to allow the story its best expression. But what if you went about it in the opposite way: first build the world, in great detail, and then find a story within that setting? This, essentially, is what Steve Beard and myself did in our collaborative novel, *Gogmagog*. Each of us took on separate roles, working in tandem to create a shared world from two very different minds. In fact, Steve often referred to the 'third mind' during the process, to describe this shared creation; an image that helped to focus our attention. This essay will describe the history of the project, specifically from a worldbuilding point of view, and will hopefully offer some insights for other writers seeking to work collaboratively.

It started when I came across a reference online to a Philippine *aswang*, a vampiric creature of folklore which uses its proboscis-like tongue to suck the blood of unborn babies out of the mother's womb while she lies asleep. A startling image. Steve and I wondered how such a creature would translate to Britain, and came up with an idea for a television horror series, featuring a detective tracking down a serial killer who steals his victims' inner organs without leaving any external wounds. The mystery is solved when the killer turns out to be a demonic figure, who pushes his extremely long, fanged tongue down people's throats, to eat at their innards. We did a fair amount of work on this, creating a cast of characters, a plot, clues, twists and turns, and a locale in present-day London. We wrote a first draft of episode one. But we struggled to make it work, not least because there have been plenty of paranormal detective stories over the years, and it's difficult to find a new approach. But this idea got us thinking about London, and its hidden lore, its darker histories, its varied cultures and peoples. We were interested in exploring that world in some further way, and eventually we decided to create our own version of the city, a fantastical or alternative London, which we could explore more freely, without any restraints; a city where we could let our imaginations go wild. And so the first bricks of Ludwich were laid.

We envisioned a vast metropolis, a capital with a great river running through it, and a whole host of different tribes and belief systems to fuel the city's narratives. But, at this early point, we did not know how best to express our ideas; would this be a feature film, a television show, a series of short stories, or a novel? At one point we considered turning it into a tabletop role-playing game. So the actual form of the city moved back and forth, through these different expressions. But all the time we were working on the central idea of the city itself, as a growing entity. Whenever we met up for coffee or to walk in the local park, we added new buildings, organisations, social strata, political intrigues, and so on. Steve has a lot of knowledge of the more esoteric tales and mythologies of London, and so we brought in elements from the life and work of the Elizabethan occultist Dr John Dee, from the numerous submerged rivers, the various secret societies. All of this was taken from our reality and translated into Ludwich, so Ludwich is a direct analogue of London, but seen through a distorting lens. This worldbuilding process was fun, and it emerged quite naturally out of our friendship, and our shared and differing interests. My personal obsession is storytelling, plain and simple, and for me Ludwich became a repository of stories, some of which we would tell, others imply, while many more remain hidden in the cellars, brothels and backroom temples of the city.

Various experiments were conducted. We swapped emails, with plans of action, maps, character names, place names, magic spells, made-up articles from the *Ludwich Scryer* newspaper. We sent each other passages from H.G. Wells, Charles Dickens, Joseph Conrad, all with their own brilliant and very atmospheric descriptions of life on and around the River Thames. But of course, we no longer had the Thames, now we had the Nysis, our river, the Ludwich river. It teemed with life, it carried far stranger cargoes than ever went up and down the Thames. To populate our city, we came up with half a dozen different tribal groups, some of them getting along just fine, others in conflict. In other words, life as it is lived. And the project grew and grew. I have more than two hundred documents in the Ludwich folder, the first dating back four years before the first words of the novel were written. We have histories of the land and the city going back to the earliest times, and onwards, through the medieval periods, up to the modern. We had both read Erich von Däniken's *Chariots of the Gods?* when we were young. This book popularised the theory that the human race had, at some point in its history, been visited by alien visitors, and that these aliens had in some way propelled us along the evolutionary pathway. The film *2001: A Space Odyssey* also utilises this story. So this too went into the Ludwich mix, as we imagined spaceships landing on the planet, and populating the earth with the first tribes. Nothing was off-limits. The period when the Ludwich project was going to be a role-playing game is perhaps the most important, as the creation of such a game involves amassing material, all possible material that might one day become a playable element, without thought for any specific narrative usage. So we wrote descriptions for each of the Ludwich tribes including their magical systems, social codes, religious beliefs, slang terms, fashion choices, even what kind of tea they liked to drink. These tribal members would be the playable characters of the game, equivalent to the wizards and warriors of Dungeons & Dragons. Steve spoke of a role-playing game being 'a tool-kit for a novel'. I loved that idea. Some years before, I had formulated a narrative method called the *grain web system*, which encouraged the collecting of individual story elements (names, characters, events, etc) on a web. This web was then rearranged into a linear story, unfolding into a plot. We were doing something very similar with Ludwich. Yet despite all these experiments, we could not settle on a perfect medium.

We had streets and alleyways, boroughs, a city, a country, a world. We lacked the final component: a story. And then one day, Steve, on an entirely different subject, mentioned he had always wanted to write a version of Joseph Conrad's *Heart of Darkness*, but set not in the past, and not in Africa, but in present-day England, a voyage up the Thames, from the estuary to the capital and onwards to the source of the river, seeing England as a semi-mystical land, a place where the old kings, old gods, still have the power to haunt us. And I replied: well, that sounds like a Ludwich story.

And so it began, the next stage of our journey. We needed a boat, we needed a captain. So much had been placed in store, yet there were always surprises along the way. I remember saying to Steve that I would like our hero, Cady Meade, to be old, in her late seventies, just because I'd never written a character of that age before. But neither of us knew at the beginning that Cady would actually turn out to be over a thousand years old, and would have a half-human, half-plant nature. Nor did we realise just how rude and earthy Cady would be: she swore her way into existence from paragraph one. Her boat was the *Juniper*, an old but still robust steam launch. The advantage of the river voyage, story-wise, is that we could now show our invented world one landscape or village at a time, as the *Juniper* passes through each region. Worldbuilding becomes much easier with such a structure, and we decided early on that we would resist as far as possible any overarching view; rather, we would put the world together piece by piece in the reader's mind, as Cady experiences it. Whatever the subject, if Cady can't see it, or think about it in memory, or talk about it to another character, then the reader will not know of it. It's a focused lens on a massive subject, showing only one section at a time. Texture is added by the mentioning of places that aren't actually visited. For instance, a number of times we hear about Tolly Hoo, Ludwich's equivalent of London's Soho district. We did have a chapter planned, where Cady would visit Tolly Hoo, but this never made it to the final draft. However, the references remain in place. This makes the world more real. Next we needed a crew for the boat, and some passengers. We made sure that each person represented a different tribe, to set the tension levels high right from the start. Finally, we were ready. The *Juniper* sets off from an island near the river's mouth, sailing up the Nysis towards Ludwich. All the years of preparation had led to this moment.

The *aswang* creature was still there, as our antagonist, hanging on from the very first inklings. But over the opening chapters of our novel, that demonic figure started to transform into something much more English in nature. Geoffrey of Monmouth was a twelfth-century cleric most famous for his chronicle, *Historia Regum Britanniae*, more commonly known as *The History of the Kings of Britain*. One of the earliest histories of the country, it contains the first ever mention of King Lear, and helped to popularise the legends of King Arthur and the Knights of the Round Table. But we were most interested in the origin myth presented in the book. Geoffrey of Monmouth possessed some knowledge of real events, but many areas were a mystery to him. So, basically, he made things up, to fill in the gaps. He conjures up a Trojan soldier called Brutus, a mercenary and a wanderer, who, under the guidance of the goddess Diana, lands with his warriors on the island of Albion. Albion was occupied at the time by a race of giants, chief among them Gogmagog. Brutus and his forces defeat the giants, and, with the death of Gogmagog, he claims the land as his own, renaming it 'Britain' after his own name. This mythmaking fascinated us, and we decided to use some of Geoffrey of Monmouth's ideas for our novel, but changing them as necessary. Gogmagog became our demon, our villain. Instead of Brutus, we chose a later king from the same chronicle, King Lud, the founder and namer of London (derived from *Caerlud*, 'Lud's fortress'). Lud, unlike Brutus and Gogmagog, has some claims to a real existence: he is both historical and mythological at the same time. Steve and I did a bit of mythmaking of our own, casting out Brutus, and instead pitting Lud against Gogmagog. This great battle became the founding myth of our city, which we now named *Ludwich*. Another component was in place. And we didn't know it at the time of first discovery, but Gogmagog would later give us the name of our novel.

Without quite realising it to begin with, we were now writing a fantasy novel. We thought it would be exciting to play with some of the tropes of the genre, but with our own particular twists added. We wanted to create something new, and fresh, while keeping true to the genre's basic themes. So now we had to ask ourselves, what sort of creature was Gogmagog, in our version of the tale? And more importantly, where were the dragons? I read an account of George R.R. Martin's first version of *A Game of Thrones*, a draft which did not include any dragons. One of his friends persuaded the author to include the legendary beasts. So that question popped into my head: where are the Ludwich dragons? Perhaps every fantasy novelist needs to ask and answer this question at some point, and make a decision about their appearance or non-appearance; and if non-appearance, then who or what replaces them? One of the most famous dragons, taken from Norse mythology, is *Jörmungandr*, also known as the Midgard Serpent, or the World Serpent. Jörmungandr is a vast sea serpent, whose body is so long he circles the entire Earth (Midgard), biting his own tail in the process, ouroboros-style. The Norse god of thunder, Thor, battles with Jörmungandr, kills him, but is wounded in the process, and poisoned with the dragon's venom. In some versions of the legend, Thor survives the battle; in other versions, he manages to walk just nine steps before falling down dead. Elements of this story certainly turn up in our novel, but more importantly for us, we were excited by this idea of a dragon encircling the world. Let's say that a great dragon did exist, that it is now dead, long dead, killed in battle, but its ghost still haunts the land; or better yet, that it haunts the river. We envisioned the dragon's ghost being sixty miles long, its whole length clinging to the River Nysis from close to the estuary, through Ludwich, and onwards to the dragon's resting place in the fields to the west of the city. This for me was the key moment, when the novel really started to take off. In preparation, I reread J.G. Ballard's *The Day of Creation*, the story of a river journey through landscapes real, psychological and hallucinatory. We could have the *Juniper* sail not only along the river, through the real landscapes of our alternative England, but also along the ghost of the dragon. In fact, let's have the boat do the entire journey, from the ghost's head to the tip of the tail, an epic adventure. All narratives follow a line, often straight and linear, sometimes broken, on occasions zigzag or circular. Ours followed the spectral curves of the ghost's body.

We gave our dragon a name, *Haakenur*. And we called its ghost *Faynr*. Gogmagog would be an opposing force, battling against Faynr for control for the capital, and the country beyond. The fight between Thor and Jörmungandr was written in the Norse legends as the final outcome of Ragnarok, the battle at the end of the world. Ragnarok pits the forces of chaos against the forces of order, with the future of the Earth and mankind in the balance. In our book, Faynr is the force of order, and Gogmagog the force of chaos. They are twin ghosts of the same body, that of Haakenur: one born of the dragon's heart, the other born of the dragon's venom. And this continuous struggle between the two ghosts takes place not on some fantastical battlefield, but against the backdrop of Ludwich; in other words, present-day London.

Or, perhaps not exactly the present day. We started to talk about setting the story in the past. Certainly, we had no interest in the quasi-medieval world of popular or traditional fantasy. We wanted to explore a period closer to our time. We considered the Victorian period, but worried about the book having too much of a steampunk atmosphere. We thought about the 1970s, a time we both know well from our youth, a decade steeped in interest regarding politics and culture. But in the end, we chose a slightly earlier period: the aftermath of the Second World War. The post-war years were a time of great societal change, of national and personal grief, of the rebuilding of the city, and of the spirit. Wounds to the old class system brought about political shifts that still affect us to this day. The loss of empire, and of faith, the new energy of the young, women moving away from traditional roles, the education of the working classes. This, then, would be our period. We settled on the year 1947, some two years after the end of the war. Details of clothing, manners, artistic movements, the way men and women act with each other, popular songs, food and drink, movie stars: everything is taken from that year, and then filtered through the fantasy lens, and transplanted into Ludwich. This process grounds the novel, allowing the fantastical elements to rise up from an absolute historical reality. We found this very useful, as whenever we got stuck, we could always ask ourselves this simple question: how would it be in 1947? However, the novel does not reveal the date 1947 to the reader. Originally, in the first draft, it did. Here's the relevant passage, in chapter five, quite a way into the story, where the year is first revealed:

Cady stood up straight, pulling herself together. The roll and rhythm of the *Juniper* did its best to mollify her. The journey was underway. It was a Thursday, the twenty-ninth of May, in the Year of our Lud, 1947.

This led to our only serious disagreement, as collaborators: I really wanted to state the year clearly; Steve didn't, he wanted to leave it ambiguous. He was worried that people would think the novel an example of the 'alternative history' genre, rather than urban fantasy. The reader would always be looking for ways of relating the book's events to real, historical facts, and its characters to real people. Rather: let the story float free. For my part, I like historical fiction. In fact, my last eight books (including *Gogmagog* and *Ludluda*, its follow-up) have all been set in the past. I like to let the reader know both *where* they are, and *when* they are. There is enough ambiguity to go round, without adding to it. So, the discussions continued. But everybody else involved in the project agreed with Steve, so in the end I relented, and the date was removed. To make this work, we needed to invent a new way of marking time, giving names to the years, rather than numbers. So the final passage now reads:

> Cady stood up straight, pulling herself together. The roll and rhythm of the *Juniper* did its best to mollify her. The journey was underway. It was a Thursday, the twenty-ninth of May, in the Year of Speculation.

We spent some time coming up with a new dating system. It works like this: the current year is always known as the Year of Speculation. At the end of the year the Council of Speculation meet to decide on the year's proper official name, depending on the major events, upheavals and glories of that year. So we have the Year of First Arrival, the Year of the Whirlpool, the Year of the Blight, the Year of Spark Fire, and so on. I will admit that the lack of a numbered date does add a layer of mystery to the novel. I wish I could inhabit readers' heads, and follow their progress as they try to set the story in a time period. It's obviously not present-day (no mobile phones!), yet when is it set, exactly? I was born in 1957, when the memories and after-effects of the war were still very much present in people's minds, and in British culture as a whole. So I know what the post-war period felt like, even if through family anecdotes and popular movies and comic books. As kids, we played at 'war', pretending to be German and English soldiers, and I constructed plastic models of Spitfires. So, if I were the reader of this book, and not one of the writers, it would be a fairly easy task for me to set the novel in that specific period. Viewed in this way, the story is slightly more real than fantastical. But to other readers, with no memories of that post-war period, the book might well be the opposite: more fantastical than real. It's interesting, either way, to consider the possibilities of interpretation. Despite my misgivings, I would certainly recommend the technique of setting a definite time period for a story, using that as a template, and then later on removing any mention of the date. The same technique can also be used for place, as well as time: London for Ludwich. One last point on this subject: the second and concluding book in the series, *Ludluda*, reveals the year 1947, but in what I think is a very surprising manner. So, we both had our way in the end. This was a true collaboration.

Another fortuitous Internet find: leeches have segmented bodies, thirty-four segments all together. So let's say that our dragon ghost also has different sections along its sixty-mile length. Each section could have a different name, a different atmosphere, each housing a different organ, and so on. On its travels, the *Juniper* will reach each section in turn and be affected in a different way each time. We have the brain, the spleen, the gallbladder, the heart, the womb, and many other regions. Cady and the other members of the crew face each new territory as best they can. We increased the sense of danger by introducing a sickness to Faynr's spectral body, so everything is far worse than it used to be. This is our version of the 'wounded land', that central trope of the fantasy novel. The narrative structure was now clear, a boat journey along the dragon's ghost, with an overarching problem and mystery involving the two passengers: who are they, what secrets are they keeping, why does Cady Meade have such a terrible sense of foreboding? Are the passengers tied in with Gogmagog's plans for dominance?

Prior to *Gogmagog* and *Ludluda*, Steve and I had written a novel together, *Mappalujo*. This was very much an experimental work, growing out of a writing game. We chose a number of famous figures from history and fiction and used these as starting points, each of us picking a name from the list, and then writing a chapter based in some way on that person's life and work. This method enabled us to have a different writing style for each chapter, thereby eliminating the central problem of the collaborative novel: how to create one authorial voice.

We knew that *Gogmagog* would be very different, much more of a linear novel, telling a more straightforward story. It needed a singular tone all the way through. We decided on the following process. First of all the creation of the world, by the two of us, as described here. Then we made an outline of the complete story, beginning to end. This was quite detailed, running to some ten pages, though, of course, we veered off track on occasions. Then we began to write. We would meet up once a week in a cafe, and discuss ideas for the upcoming chapter, deciding on character motivations, events, lines of dialogue, etc. I would take copious notes. Then I went home and started to write. I can write quickly. I would aim to finish a chapter or a good portion of a chapter in four or five days, which I would then send to Steve. I wasn't at all concerned here with getting it 'right', or with producing polished writing, but more with keeping the story flowing onwards. Steve would send me notes, sometimes very detailed notes on the chapter, and I would put these into place. I tended to always go with his suggestions. Then we started work on the next chapter.

In quite a short period of time we produced a first draft. We then worked extensively on this, looking at character development, plotting, suspense, narrative tension, consistency of style and theme; in other words, all the standard tasks of a second draft. In this way, the novel was built, as the world was built: word by word, brick by brick. And then we did the whole thing a second time, for the follow-up novel, *Ludluda*, which brings Cady's epic battle against Gogmagog to its conclusion at the burial site of the great dragon, Haakenur.

To an artist of the twentieth century, a 'found object' was an actual object; nowadays we browse the Internet and pick up images and strange facts along the way. A Philippine vampire, a twelfth-century cleric with a wild imagination, an interview with the author of *A Song of Ice and Fire*, a Norse myth about a world-spanning serpent, the magical diagrams and mirrors of John Dee, Conrad's African odyssey, UFO sightings, the anatomy of the leech. All these things were part and parcel of Ludwich, its planning and subsequent development. We stayed alert, ever hopeful of new things to add all the way through the process: the building of a city, the mapping of a river's route, the unfolding of a story that enabled us to explore that city and that river, from sea to source, from ruined docklands to high temple, from the dragonhead to the bones of the fallen serpent, and finally to the vast half-buried skull and the mystery of what lies within the dragon's hollowed-out eye. As the journey concludes, the Year of Speculation finally achieves its proper name: *Becoming*. Both noun and verb; may it ever be so.

What I Think About When I Think About Reality

Alex Pheby

When I was growing up, we had a black cat. I think my parents got him when I was a baby, and he died in my first year at university, so there wasn't really a time when I lived at home that he didn't live with me. His given name was David, but I called him Puss and I knew what he looked like very clearly.

One day, when I was about ten probably – I don't remember – he hadn't come home for his dinner, and I thought he was probably dead. I went to look for him in the woods on the verge of the playing fields down the road from where we lived; he'd go there to hunt the mice he'd leave on my pillow every now and then.

It was late autumn, twilight, my vision wasn't great and for various reasons I didn't have glasses. In the hour or so I looked for him I saw his corpse at least three times. Each time the sight was very precise and unusually detailed; more so than the backs of my hands on the keyboard as I type these words. I saw him, his neck bent back, open-mouthed, one eye lost, every aspect vivid enough to catch my breath. Except I didn't see any of it, because when I went closer he was just a mossy branch lying in the undergrowth. Then, a little bit later, he was hanging from a tree, killed by local kids and strung up. Again, not though, because that was a black bin liner caught on a branch. Then he was lying flattened from a car accident, his fur matted with blood and half buried in the dirt. That time he was a lost bobble hat.

In each experience I was anxiously mistaken, but the visual impression was very exact, even as I walked warily to where I expected to find him. He only became something else when I came close enough, magically transforming out of his dead body.

When it eventually got dark, and I went home, there he was curled up on my bed.

I don't doubt that an optometrist, a psychiatrist, a neurologist could provide a rational account of how and why this came about – I can think of a few myself – but at that time, in that place, and for me, it felt as if, between the conscious acts of looking and the conscious recognition of the visual impressions, there was an unconscious mediation of those impressions, a kind of pattern recognition/image substitution that took place outside of my control in a space and time somewhere between my eyes and my mind.

What mechanism was doing that mediating work?

Under what conditions?

If my senses were being mediated, what did that mean for my understanding of the real? What did it mean for my perception of reality to be liable to influence from flaws in my senses, from my anxiety, from my imagination? Why did this doubting of my ability to understand the world give me a particular feeling in my stomach and behind my teeth, a kind of ache or itch?

Fast forward to me at thirty, and I was working as a cataloguer at the library of the University of North London, now London Metropolitan University. That library hadn't as yet devolved responsibility for cataloguing their new books to a central authority, so it was my job, in part, to read enough of the books that came in to work out where they should be shelved. Generally this didn't take long – a page or two – but one day I picked up from the pile Daniel Paul Schreber's *Memoirs of My Nervous Illness*, which is an unusually detailed and rational autobiographical account of the hallucinations of a judge from Wilhelmine Germany who was suffering from schizophrenia. Schreber wrote his memoir while he was held against in his will in an asylum, and it was written as a means of securing his release, outlining how his experiences – very briefly, he believed his and God's nerves had been entangled and that now he was drawing God down to earth, something God was resisting by attacking him with miracles – were of the same order of experience as everyone else's experiences. He felt that he was entirely in charge of his faculties, and capable of managing his own affairs even if he believed, as he also claimed, that God had scoured the world of human beings and was turning him into a woman.

It wasn't that difficult a book to categorise – somewhere in the 616.89 area – but by lunchtime I was still reading it, and I eventually ended up writing a PhD thesis on Schreber, part of which was published as my second novel *Playthings*. Why this is relevant here is that, like my own mistakings of the world, Schreber's experiences, no matter how fantastical they might seem, no matter how incorrect, were subjectively entirely real, at least temporarily. Also, his treatment of these unreal reals in writing was sufficient to convince the authorities that he was, in fact, rational enough that he ought to be released from the asylum and allowed to return home, even though he never disavowed the reality of his experiences

The experience of reading Schreber produced that same ache in the stomach, the same itch behind the teeth that I'd got looking for my cat.

Why?

Why did I also get that feeling with certain types of art, particularly surrealism?

Why did I get it taking the shortcut to my bedsit across Streatham Park late at night when the lights were off?

And on waking somewhere unfamiliar?

* * *

By and large, I don't like to be mistaken about things all the time; I prefer to be right about the world. I don't like to be anxious all the time; I prefer to be relaxed. I don't like uncertainty; I prefer to be certain. I might like any and all of these things in short, contained, controllable doses, but I don't like to be at the mercy of them. To be at the mercy of them I consider a disease of my mind.

The material realities I surround myself with, it seems to me, are designed to minimise mistakes, anxiety, and uncertainty that might lead me to question the reality of the world.

When I walk down a street near my home, I find that I know what everything is – either specifically, or generally, or both – without any effort. There is my house, there is another house in the same style, there is a car, there is my car, there is the road I drive my car on, there is the roundabout. If I keep walking, my specific recognition of the world lessens, but my general understanding compensates. There is a street like my street, there are cars like my car, this road is like the road I drive on.

Eventually I stray out of my real if I walk for long enough. The familiar geometries of the human built environment – rectangles and cubes, circles and spheres, lines – are replaced by the countryside. Mostly, though, this place has been divided up into familiar shapes too – rectangular fields, lines of dividing hedgerow, the orderly shapes of agricultural buildings. Still, I start to become uneasy, start to feel that particular feeling in my stomach and behind my teeth. It's a bit like dread, a bit like fear, but not it's quite either. I look at all the rectangles, all the reassuringly flat and defined contours of things, and imagine them on a map, replacing reality with the algebra of cartography.

If I still feel uncomfortable, I need only turn around, go back towards home, for my safe understanding of the world to come back to me. In the place of the dread-like, fear-like feeling, there is an absence of it that feels like something else. Comfortableness? Certainty? Whatever it is, it is this feeling about the world, the feeling of being certain in my knowledge that signals, at least partially, the presence of reality for me.

I wear glasses now, have my phone to hand, go to places where things support my feeling of being certain in my real, places that people like me have made to make people like me feel comfortable. I watch this same real in my entertainments, read about this real in books, even write about it, sometimes.

This real is built about me, and even if I step out of it, I do so knowing I can return, and the other things and places, the other feelings, are temporary. Any unreals are just that – unreal.

Except, sometimes, even when I'm in the real that has been so carefully constructed around me, that has been curated for my comfort, that I know and accept and rely on, I still feel uncomfortable in it.

Perhaps I've read too much German idealist philosophy, too much about solipsism, too much about post-structuralism, went to too many exhibitions of surrealism, of Dada, of symbolism, became too focused on stories where people were oppressed by the fragility of their reals. Perhaps I can blame Franz Kafka and Angela Carter, Georges Bataille and Octavia Butler.

Perhaps I need therapy...

...but some of the time it seems to me that reality is not some solid, comfortable, agreeable thing, but is instead an anxious, plastic, infinitely malleable place that only feels certain because we all go to a lot of effort to make sure that it does, and even then it's not entirely convincing. Out of the corner of my eye, particularly when I'm somewhere I don't usually go, or when it's dark, or when I'm not wearing my glasses, or when I'm ill, I can see the real before it's mediated for me: the formless, senseless mass that pattern and thought and architecture shapes into the things I recognise. I can sense it before I understand it.

It makes my stomach ache and my teeth itch.

When that happens, I start to wonder whether the world is undifferentiated and formless until it meets perception, and that we make the world from chaos through a kind of magic, transforming the base and meaningless material of the universe into specific things through pattern creation and recognition, through language, through mathematics. I think of the faces I've seen in the outlines of clouds, the fighting animals in Rorschach tests, the movement in static optical illusions. If we make the world rather than experience it, what does it mean for something to be real?

Then I start thinking about Puss and about Schreber.

What differentiates, qualitatively, my subjective experience of my mistakes in perception and hallucinations from the subjective experiences I have of the real that I don't think are mistaken or hallucinated?

And what about collective psychological states that determine what we agree is real, but which change through history?

What about collective delusions like fascism?

What about ideologies in general?

What about ideologies that we don't realise now are ideologies, but which future generations will recognise as ideological?

What of culture?

What of custom?

What if the mistakes I make about my real are more widespread than I realise?

My stomach aches and my teeth itch, but it's not just the possibility of my subjective real being unstable that worries me when I think about these things. What if everyone's real is equally unstable? What is 'the real' in general if everyone's subjective real is questionable?

Well, I think, the real is that thing which is agreed to be the real, taking into account all of the above.

But who is doing the agreeing? Not people like Schreber, presumably. Not me, when I'm tired.

Aren't lots of people excluded from agreeing what constitutes the real? Children are excluded, often, as are those with mental illnesses. Some religious people. People who believe in ghosts. Lots of people whose identities are marginalised though ethnicity, gender, class, sexuality, ability, neurotypicality. Even political opinions can exclude you. Anyone can be excluded from the real whose perception of it differs significantly from some presumed and accepted consensus.

And what is this consensus anyway?

Did I miss the meeting where it was agreed?

Is it scientists who decide what the real is? If it is, then it's a very odd form of consensus, because I've never met a scientist who'd agree to define it.

Do philosophers decide it? If they do, they don't seem to agree with each other either. And very few of us listen to them anymore.

But, Alex, you know it when you see it, though, right?

Well... I'm not sure I do. I get stomach aches, and my teeth itch.

What if all the so-called real things in my life are immaterial phantoms contained by my mind, or conjured for me by a hateful God – as Schreber believed – or that I'm living in a simulation. Perhaps reality is a comfortable fantasy that keeps worrying thoughts like this at bay. The world is knowable, I tell myself, it's stable, I share it with everyone.

It's real!

Look, there's a house, a car, a road!

But what if this real is something I make up for myself – that we make up for ourselves – to keep stomach ache and tooth itch at bay? What if the real real is the uncertain, unstable, formless chaos of the universe within which we find ourselves, and which we hide behind illusions of certainty, shared experience, and facts?

Is it this formless real that we attempt to remove from our adult lives with the fantasised 'reality', relegating the other real to a failure to understand our senses, or to hallucinatory anxiety? We create worlds around us that are very easily recognised and understood: road signs, civic architecture, a whole menagerie of manufactured objects with which we fill our senses, making environments we can be certain of immediately.

Why do we need to do that, if the real is so real?

What if these environments require us to act in particular ways for their reality to be maintained? What if they require the constant performance of roles within these environments in order to keep them real? Designated tasks in designated places, in designated clothes – the banker's suit, the doctor's coat, the office worker's smart casual attire?

And when we get home, where we change into the clothes proper to the subcultures we identify with, aren't we still surrounded by our constructed reals?

And all this depending on systems and assumptions we scarcely understand, but must faithfully take for real – global free market economics, fiat currency exchange, monetarism – performing the rituals underpinned by complex systems vouched for by priesthoods of economists, bankers, politicians.

The real, as it is made by these rituals, seems to require endless and neurotic repetition in the architecture of the built environment, whether that is the industrial estate, the high street, the central business district, low-rise warehouses, high-rise investment banks, in clothing, in waking in time for the nine-to-five, in the commute, in the after-work drinks, in the life/work balance, in the masculine, in the feminine, in all of the costumed rituals of the capitalist real.

Are these any more real than the rituals of the past, which we see now for the temporary, historical, arbitrary pretences they always were?

We act as if we have reached the end of history, found the real real that the generations of the past failed to find. Even as we live through decade after decade of unparalleled change, ever accelerating, we double down on the idea of the reality of the real.

Our real.

But, again, what of those whose lives are outside of this real, who are not invited to join? Do they, then, live in strange and unknowable fictions we are not obliged to treat as real? What of the unacceptable and distant reals of the radicalised, the illegal, the esoteric? The magical worlds of people who believe differently to the parochial certainties of our real of backwater, obedient, tedious mundanities? Our embroidered outrages and manufactured passions, provided to ourselves, by ourselves, as a poor substitute for connection with each other and which are immediately and flimsily appropriated for the profit of organisations which have long since outrun their founders, long since outrun their functions, and now operate in a fevered feedback loop providing uncountable numbers in valueless currencies for no one?

It's then that I think that perhaps the ache in my stomach, the itch in my teeth, aren't the signs of existential anxiety. Perhaps instead it's a kind of anticipation, a kind of excitement at the opening up of new and better possibilities for the real.

Reals reliant on rituals and repetition are prone to mutation, and the system that seems to us so solid and real now, so inescapable, might have no foundation: its laws might be nonsenses, temporary attempts to anchor reality, to pin it down, where it cannot be pinned down. Any successes in making reality might only be temporary, and though any resistance might also only be temporary and any new and better real would also only be temporary, the forms of the real are made by us, for us: we might only need to make space in which we can understand what to do with them.

Then I think that, during periods in which our real seeks to deny its contingency, seeks to work against the people of the world and to close down the possibilities of alternative reals,

I – we – should work to destabilise certainty in the real, to de-stabilise realisms, and to become, to borrow a term from entre-preneurial capitalism, disruptors of the real.

It seems then that it's important to understand that, despite appearances, we might be in a period in which the antithesis of capitalism is on the rise. Change is being resisted by ideological and repressive apparatuses in an attempt to drain the last dregs of value from a dying economic system. Progressive energies are being co-opted, as they always have been, by conservative forces aiming to escape the inevitable, which is that this system is failed.

Then I start thinking about what that means for me as a writer.

Perhaps the central problem of representative realism, for me, is that it represents something passing, almost passed, and there is a need for me to summon up a new world, to bring into existence reals that will exceed and surpass the banal and valueless nonsenses from which we are emerging.

Isn't realism, at times like now, regressive? There will come a time, hopefully soon, when realism will be required again to represent new reals into which we are emerging, but for now, it operates in the service of a dying system, reifying something that is ceasing to exist but which still has sufficient power to take us all with it.

Of course, I tell myself, realist representation can call the real into question, can alter it, can transform it, but isn't this transformation a kind of fantasising? A kind of magical thinking? A break with the real?

Then what does that mean for genre? I can't possibly argue that SFF eludes the grip of capitalism – it demonstrably doesn't – but there are progressive possibilities for fantastic writing in the destabilisation of the real, however brief, through which new reformulations of the real may be provoked. This is possible within realism, but not within capitalist realism – as Mark Fisher defined it – nor is it as integral to the project of realism as it is to writing that constructs worlds that differ from the real but must, in order for them to be taken seriously, be read as reals.

This, I think, is the problem a lot of literary criticism has in its approach to unreal reals, and to fantasy fiction in particular: it ignores the effect that taking an unreal as real has in opening up an understanding that all real creation is intrinsically unreal.

It does not seem to me, in those moments, to be accidental that even the most commercial forms of fantasy, science fiction and horror are where queer, trans, and politically transformational work are taking place.

* * *

Writing things like this provokes that feeling in my stomach, and behind my teeth. It makes me feel a little ill, a little vulnerable. It makes me think I'm making mistakes, that I'm misunderstanding the real. Perhaps I'm a morbid and irrational thinker, mistaking the world entirely.

One of my thesis supervisors when I was doing my PhD was Professor Lyndsey Stonebridge, who currently holds the

Interdisciplinary Chair of Humanities and Human Rights at Birmingham University and who I respect enormously. Her latest book is a biography of Hannah Arendt, the philosopher and historian, and she was interviewed about it at the Bruno Kreisky Forum for International Dialogue, a video of which I watched on YouTube last year.[1] I advise you to watch it, not because it has much bearing on what I've been writing, but because it makes me realise how little of what I think about the real has to do with truth, which is a very important concept that I don't properly understand.

There's part of the interview where Lyndsey – I think of her as Lyndsey, not Professor Stonebridge, but even that feels uncomfortable – is talking about being in a post-truth world. She says a lot of interesting and important things, all of which I agreed with while I was watching it, but she also made me feel tense. I don't really have a conclusion to this essay, any more than my thoughts when I think about reality have a conclusion, but in a post-truth world it seems to me that it's no longer truth that's the issue – the battle to save truth, at least for progressive forces, has already been lost. It is certainty, it seems to me, that is central; particularly the false certainty with which certain reals are taken as true.

Certainties are useful, but they are also dangerous. They prevent you from being able to see the world as other people see it. They overwrite the formless real with images of the things you think and that you fear – you'll remember my dead cat from earlier. Arendt wrote on the Nuremberg Trials, amongst

---

1   www.youtube.com/watch?v=UOzOxD54dmo

other things. Certainties allow people to industrialise murder. They allow you to ruin the world and everything in it.

People would never do things so terrible if they weren't certain they were right to do them.

It seems to me that certainty is a psychological remnant of a time when a real could be agreed on, and while it is tempting to co-opt this feeling from the grand narratives that have been overturned – it feels like a kind of revenge on fascism, a kind of inheritance of its power, a kind of victory – it is a co-option that is always already prone to violence.

There is no transcendental real – no fixed, reliable, comfortable world. The fantasies of a real of this kind are the dreams of dead systems. They were never what they were imagined to be, only corrupted and contingent truths vouchsafed by power, by violence.

There is no real for realism to represent; there are just fantasies.

This is what I think about when I think about reality.

Sometimes: my next book is a return to literary fiction, to non-existent realism, so I'll see what I think after that's finished.

SPOTLIGHT ON...
MICHAEL MOORCOCK

How Beautiful They Are: *Elric of Melniboné* and the Amoral Elf Motif

J.L. Worrad

The Dragon Isle

What is it with beautiful yet amoral civilisations? Why are we, fantasy readers, drawn to their sinuous towers and decadent arts? Why do we swoon over their equally beautiful yet amoral citizens and that way they dance in the face of decay?

It's a trope that runs through the history of genre fiction and I bloody love it. Hell, as a fantasy author I drink from its well all the time. But, the more I dwell on it, the more I realise all these florid and grotesque roads lead back to fabled Imrryr.

Imrryr, the Dreaming City, capital of Melniboné, the dragon

isle. Even this sentence, composed as it is of chewed-up parts I've haplessly spewed into rough order, evokes wonder and mystery. Michael Moorcock's creations forever wear the finery of his well-chosen names. That's the first thing I noticed on going back to his 1972 novel *Elric of Melniboné*: its power to evoke.

Elric of Melniboné is a jewel. There's an adage in genre reading circles with regards to coming back to a once-cherished book after many years: 'the Word Goblins got to it'. Your tastes have refined and your reading has widened and the work your teenage self revered is now so unspeakably, laughably poor the only explanation is malevolent spirits have cursed every paragraph in the intervening years. Not so *Elric of Melniboné*. It repels Word Goblins like Immryr's coastal death-maze repels marauders. Fiction marches on, of course, and it probably wouldn't be published these days. But neither would *The Lord of the Rings* or *The Golden Ass*. The Parthenon with its stately grace endures. Only a fool would ask if it's fitted with a smart meter.

Like many British Generation X-ers, I came to Elric by way of *White Dwarf*, Games Workshop's in-house magazine. Back then, *White Dwarf* was less an eighty-page advertisement for GW's wares and more a nerd's bazaar, an interzone for the diverse and nascent fantasy gaming world and, by extension, the fantasy genre entire. It even had a book review feature, Critical Mass, by the inimitable David Langford of *Ansible* fame, which seems improbable now. Chaosium, the company who created *Call of Cthulhu*, were riding high with *Stormbringer*, a role-playing game set in the world of Elric, and Games Workshop not only sold the game in their shops but also crafted *Stormbringer*'s miniatures. The advertisement for them in *White Dwarf* had my twelve-year-old mind resolutely hooked. There was the look of these figurines, of course, so lithe and sinister. In retrospect, these Melnibonéans were the clear prototype for Warhammer's high elves, not least the albino emperor himself with his tall helm and flowing locks. But really it was the names that beguiled me: 'Dyvim Tvarr', 'Tanglebones', 'Smyrna Baldhead'. From the magazine's scant descriptions, I knew Elric was somehow fuelled by his sword; that he had killed his lover (a fact that presumably nettled him); that Melniboné itself was strange and dragon-drenched. I had to know more.

I took out a copy of *Elric of Melniboné* from Syston public library. A cursory glance at Wikipedia suggests it was a first edition, so maybe I should have kept it, fines be damned. One of the things I noticed then and is marvellous to the writer I am now is the vibrant imagery. *Elric* is a fantasy novel double-dipped in colour: the ruby throne; the thousand towers of Imrryr, each its own hue; Cymoril's blue dress in a glade of blue blossoms; all of it stark upon a dark backdrop of brooding gloom. Like his friend J.G. Ballard, Moorcock is an intensely visual writer, something I never see commented upon, and I feel a need to go a little off topic and point it out. Moorcock himself talks overtly on the matter: '(My) fantasies are always thoroughly worked out,' he says in his introduction to a graphic novel of *Elric of Melniboné*, in what I like to think of as a coherent pictorial vocabulary:

This is singularly important (when writing) fantasy books in less than a week and frequently within three days. Everything must be 'in tune' – there must be an internal logic of images, just as in dreams. This much, I think, I learned from the surrealists.

The Lord of the Rings needed twelve years to be written – and decades to ferment – but *Elric of Melniboné* could only ever have been created inside of a month. It is feverish, full of hallucination and leaping electric thoughts, as bubbling and wild and fierce as the Boiling Sea to Melniboné's south-east. The iconic power of Melniboné, that decadent kingdom of fluorescent tower and slumbering dragon, of courtly dance and artful torture, lies in that frenzy of creation.

And I loved it. The phrase 'formative reading experience' is a little overused, but let's just say this and *Nineteen Eighty-Four* loomed over my early teens like the Ministry of Love over Airstrip One. Both laid the foundation to my attitudes towards reading – and later, writing – genre fiction. Perhaps the starkest testament to my admiration for Elric was that, with Games Workshop's Warhammer coming into its pomp, it was the dark elves I chose as my faction. I simply had to. They were the closest thing to Melnibonéans.

Fear of Tolkien

Elves – that is, the elves of Tolkien, of Rivendell and Lothlórien and thereabouts – are really quite creepy. With their beauty, their purity and their superiority, they simply repel some base part of the mind when thought about for too long.

Moorcock did, I suspect. Melniboné is a critique of the elven motif as Tolkien portrays it, being a twisted reflection and, to some extent, a parody, as Elric himself is on one level a twisted reflection and parody of Robert E. Howard's Conan the Cimmerian. For a start, Melnibonéans do not think of themselves as human; and, for that matter, neither does humanity. The Melnibonéans are beautiful beings, noble and graceful and steeped in an ancient heritage of high magic. Yet they lack conventional morality. Melniboné is not just the habitation of non-humans, it is an *inhuman* place, a place no human should be.

Michael Moorcock famously criticised *The Lord of the Rings* in his essay 'Epic Pooh', from 1978 (an essay that, to my tastes, has been marred by his insistence on going back and adding to it sometime in the 2000s with references to Rowling and Pratchett that not only dislocate 'Epic Pooh' from its time and place but also make it feel dated twice over). Early on, he discusses Tolkien's 'good' places: 'The little hills and woods of the Surrey of the mind, the Shire, are "safe", but the wild landscapes beyond the shire are "dangerous". Experience of life itself is dangerous.' From this viewpoint, this 'safe' and 'unsafe', Rivendell and Lothlórien are just the Shire with another face, albeit more sombre and aware of the world, Tolkien's fantasy Oxford and Cambridge to the Shire of his Worcestershire upbringing. Melniboné is an inversion of Tolkien's assumptions. The streets and towers – especially the towers – of the dreaming city are where the danger resides. It's the lands beyond where any hope of safety truly lies.

Really, what is Rivendell? A clean and sexless place, a sterilised utopia with its surplus of trees yet no dirt nor rot. The human spirit can never abide a utopia; it's why images of heaven are vague and identical while hell is mapped in countless ways. There's something about those fair and noble elf folk, something disquieting in an early-to-mid twentieth century kind of way. I mean, if you asked a fascist back then to describe their idealised future, one centuries after their 'struggle' was long done with, it would be something like Rivendell: a happy folk at one with nature, each a flawless craftsman, clean limbed and free from infirmity, each more beautiful than a sunrise. Pure fantasy, in other words, and one quite loathsome if you peer beneath the shimmering surface.

Melniboné is what you get when you dive through that surface entirely. It's no wonder Alan Moore calls it 'an antimatter antidote to Middle Earth, a toxic and fluorescing elf-repellent'. We learn of the Dreaming City's rituals upon an emperor's death:

Naked, the Dragon Princes would prowl the city, taking any young woman they found... for it was traditional that if an emperor died then the nobles of Melniboné must create as many children of aristocratic blood as was possible. Music-slaves would howl from every tower. Other slaves would be slain and some eaten. It was a dreadful dance, the dance of misery, and it took as many lives as it created.

Melniboné is tradition manifest and for Moorcock tradition is a species of madness. The Tolkienian elf reveres and maintains ancient lore, the Moorcockian elf terrorises with it.

This impulse to write about evil elves, to foul the archetype, is a healthy one. The modern author approaching the Tolkienian elf can do little else but twist them. Well, aside from choose to humanise them, which only renders the attempt pointless. Perhaps one of the more famous portrayals of amoral elvishness is Terry Pratchett's trans-dimensional variety in *Lords and Ladies*, but even Tolkien ended up creating a few individual examples with *The Silmarillion* (not that I've read it, I'll admit). A good author must always look the notions of purity and superiority in the mouth, their dental tools at the ready. The reader deserves as much.

Those Ghosts Who Ruled Him

An island nation with a bustling capital that was once the centre of a vast, warlike, racially supremacist naval empire, one that was and is unafraid of enacting terroristic atrocities upon its colonial subjects and rules its lower classes with a disdainful fist.

You can see the punchline a mile away, can't you?

Britain had lost all real claim to empire by the time the first Elric story saw print, which was June 1961 in *Science Fantasy Magazine*. The Suez crisis had played out some seven years prior, that wake-up call to a small island that it was no longer the world's policeman. Another, younger kingdom (so to speak) had taken up the role, having applied pressure to

Blighty's dusty, ration-book husk. It's no marvel that Britain's most popular comic actor at that time, Tony Hancock, played a pompous yet clueless figure: he was the nation made flesh. Even the Oxbridge intelligentsia, in the form of Peter Cook's Establishment Club, *Beyond the Fringe* and *Private Eye*, had taken to slinging satirical barbs at every venerable target. *Elric of Melniboné* was an end product of all that, a grim sibling to *Monty Python's Flying Circus*, both emerging at the rear-end of the Sixties and mixing psychedelia with rage at the status quo.

Reduced in power, Elric's homeland finds solace in dreams: 'Even the meanest slaves chewed berries to bring them oblivion and thus were easily controlled, for they came to depend on their dreams.' I'm reminded of the prolefeed in *Nineteen Eighty-Four*, the mass-produced entertainments ensuring the proles' myopic compliance. But, of course, by the Sixties, Britain had far more insidious and luminous ways to ensnare the mind than magic berries, mostly emanating from the corner of the living room.

I may be labouring the point with all this but, honestly, I only saw the metaphor this time around. The thirteen-year-old me missed the satire of British nationalism inherent to *Elric of Melniboné*, and I have to wonder whether that was due to my age or the decade I grew up in or the suburban conservatism that surrounded me. Perhaps a little of all three. Here was a unique critique of my nation – a quite blatant one – and I overlooked it entirely. 'These are the people of Melniboné, the dragon isle, which ruled the world for ten thousand years and has ceased to rule it for five hundred. And they are cruel and clever and to them "morality" means little more than a proper respect for the traditions of a hundred centuries.' Elegium pro Britannia, to quote *Withnail & I*, a work that shares a similar tone and worldview to *Elric*, at least to my mind.

> Some claimed this silver emperor who conversed with humans as if they were equals... would bring the empire down. (...) Elric's succession would cause the defences of Imrryr to tumble, they said. He would allow the human hordes to flood in. These hordes had grown powerful and longed to sack the city of the Dragon Lords... they longed to loot, to destroy, to rape.

To hold yourself up as the most glorious land, you have to perceive all other lands as lesser. You must eternally fear a loss of glory, a loss of identity, and see diversity as another word for extinction. Outsiders can enter Melniboné, but only if they make themselves useful and quiet. Even then they must accept a slow and winding voyage through the city's defensive labyrinth, which is about as clear a metaphor as any magical object can be in fantasy literature.

The Doctor Jest scene in Elric is pretty infamous in genre circles with its torture, its act of castration and the ultimate reduction of humans to meat, but it's scant different from the acts performed on suspected Mau Mau rebels in Kenya back in 1952, save for the playful and louche irony surrounding it. Of course, Moorcock knew nothing of those real-life crimes, the details only truly emerging in the mid-2000s during compensation hearings, but satirical fantasy has a way of diagnosing hitherto unseen maladies.

Most tellingly of all, Elric watches Doctor Jest's savage performance rather absentmindedly, as no doubt the United Kingdom watched colonial 'disquiet' on the evening news.

Red Mutant Eyes Gazed Down on Hunger City

He looks down the long flight of quartz steps to where his Court disports itself, dancing with such delicacy and whispering grace that it might be a court of ghosts. Mentally he debates moral issues and in itself this activity divides him from the great majority of his subjects.

It's no accident that in this secondary world, alive with so many colours, the main character is an albino. Elric's albinism is of a kind far beyond the albinism seen with humans in our world, albinism being only a jump-off point for our mind's eye into a paleness far more complete and decidedly more abstract. Elric is oil-paint white from hair to skin and he wears only black clothes and armour. The only colour lent him are two piercing eyes of a redness compared to 'crimson stones'; again, nothing like the eyes of an albino person in real life. Elric stands out from his world. Indeed, he stands out from the very pages of his book. With Moorcock, colour *is* theme. Elric is a man divorced from his culture, incapable of performing the required mental gymnastics to be truly one with his society. But he is still part of it. He is still Melnibonéan.

All fiction about a decadent and amoral civilisation, especially those of an elven or quasi-elven bent, has a main character at odds with their culture, which is to say they are experiencing some moral flux. We have it with Drizzt Do'Urden in R.A Salvatore's Dark Elf Trilogy and, if you'll forgive the self-insert, my own novel *Pennyblade* is founded entirely on the concept.

Elric of Melinboné stands as the pinnacle of that trope, and is, to mix metaphor, the very root. Elric's character arc is one of being consumed by his choices. They consume him and, increasingly as his saga continues, the world entire.

The Dreaming City, Elric's first appearance in print, was published in 1961, and his first run of stories continues throughout that decade. The Albino Emperor is a child of the Sixties, and it's hard not to see his development as being in lockstep with the emergent idea of the rock star. Michael Moorcock had long embedded himself in Britain's nascent rock scene, was friends with (and even deemed an 'auxiliary' member of) space rock pioneers Hawkwind, and his fiction was in frantic conversation with the counterculture, from the beatnik prose of Jack Kerouac and the then in vogue theatre of Brecht to the later psychedelic era of the mid-Sixties with its proliferation of LSD and the subsequent storming of perception's gates. Elric, to quote Alan Moore again, is 'bad like Gene Vincent, sick like Lenny Bruce and haunted by addiction like Bill Burroughs… as much a symbol of the times as demonstrations at the US embassy at Grosvenor Square, or Jimi Hendrix, or the Oz trial'.

Indeed, it was far from a one-way street with Elric, and from the Sixties through to the mid-Seventies a feedback loop was in effect as much as at any Stooges concert. The developing fictional character that was Elric absorbed the cultural radiation blasting out from that new post-war icon, the British rock star, particularly the cool, aloof and nigh-otherworldly variety, then fed it back into the zeitgeist and, via that (or by the more intravenous method of a cheap paperback), to the Mick Jaggers and Robert Plants and David Bowies of our world, the living Elrics.

"'I worried more for myself than for Cymoril and I called that 'morality'," thought the albino. "I tested my sensibilities, not my conscience."' Elric's conscience is a sincere yet manufactured thing, one he barely understands himself and, within *Elric of Melniboné* at least, its slow and stuttering growth is compelling to witness. It's the character arc Bowie's Thin White Duke never got to have. Elric lives in contrast to his culture, and yet at the same time fears being lost to that contrast. He is at once agitated and comforted by his own coldness.

'Mentally he debates moral issues,' Chapter One's opening tells us, 'and in itself this issue divides him from the great majority of his subjects, for these people are not human.'

Elric's cousin Yyrkoon not only serves as the antagonist of *Elric of Melniboné* but also as its default Melnibonéan, a kind of control subject in the book's investigation of ethics. Yyrkoon is baroquely amoral, hungry to kill his emperor as soon as providence allows and happy enough to marry his own sister, apparently just to cause torment to both her and her lover Elric. Yyrkoon is an entirely flat character prone to melodramatic outbursts and unthinking connivances, true, but really he's an archetype, a mask, and he serves the plot and story well enough. He's no hypocrite, though, so he has that going for him. His increasing degeneracy, interestingly, often mirrors Elric's philosophising. 'We Melnibonéans judge nothing sane nor insane,' Yyrkoon, high on sorcery and lack of sleep, tells Cymoril. 'What a man is – he is. What a man does – he does.' Meanwhile, Elric observes to a loyal friend:

> One can only judge oneself by one's actions. I have looked at what I have done, not at what I meant to do thought I would like to do, and what I have done has, in the main, been foolish, destructive and with little point.

They have come to similar conclusions, and Elric is quick to acknowledge they are the reflection of one another: 'Yyrkoon was right to despise me and that was why I hated him so.'

Elric's morality, or his earnest pretence of such, acts as an increasingly destabilising force to those around him. It's almost an infection, a memetic virus, that delivers unease to any Melnibonéan who contracts it. One such is Dyvim Tvar, Lord of the Dragon Caves and Elric's most trusted aide, perhaps even friend: 'Dyvim Tvar began to feel the burden of Elric's conscience settling upon him also. It was a peculiar feeling to come to a Melnibonéan and Dyvim Tvar knew very well that he liked it not at all.'

These increasing feelings lead Dyvim to visit his children before setting off with Elric on his search for Cymoril, children of women he almost never visits. His visit only succeeds in making everyone uncomfortable and mystified, including himself. It's a captivating scene, one helped by Dyvim being the most well-drawn character in the book save Elric, and it raises an equally captivating philosophical question: is gifting the immoral with morality itself an immoral act? For if you could give, say, a criminal psychopath the empathy they have always lacked, their sudden remorse would be a fresh and overpowering agony. It would be sheer cruelty, surely, giving them that, whatever your original intentions. A fascinating paradox, one the author uses the fantasy motif of the decadent civilisation to explore.

At the end of *Elric of Melniboné*, Elric has his throne and his lover back, not to mention the good will of his people, yet his morality, so alien to his kind, compels him to leave and learn more of the wider world. But is his morality revealed here for the artifice it actually is? After all, Cymoril, who has suffered more than anyone in this tale save the dead, clearly needs Elric to remain beside her. His nation needs him, but instead he drops it in the palm of Yyrkoon, which is a pleasing plot conclusion but objectively dangerous as a plan, especially to all of Elric's friends. It seems after so many tribulations our young emperor has failed to escape his initial flaw: he tests his sensibilities, not his conscience.

Elric talks of changing Melniboné on his return: 'For I think Melniboné must change if it is to survive. She could become a great force for good in the world, for she still has much power.' As a reader, I wonder about this. How might the Elric cycle have played out if he had indeed returned and attempted as much? We'd have a fantasy classic about a struggle to turn a decadent ancient civilisation around and find some redemption from its blood-drenched imperialist history. I don't think anything in fantasy literature has quite explored that idea in such a way, and it could have made for a fascinating series. But maybe I'm naive. Maybe fantasy can only be stretched so far.

No Mask!

Elric owes something to the aestheticism and decadent movements of the late nineteenth century (and a little beyond). Des Esseintes, for instance, the detached protagonist of Huymans' *A Rebours*, could be a louche blueprint for Elric, and it's impossible not to see hints of Carcosa in Melniboné, that arcane city of Robert W. Chambers' *The King in Yellow*, whose sleek towers rise up behind black stars in a twin-mooned sky. Within this city-within-a-play-within-a-book, the inhabitants lounge all wan and forlorn until a masked visitor breaks the routine serenity:

> Camilla: You, sir, should unmask.
> Stranger: Indeed?
> Cassilda: Indeed it's time. We all have laid aside disguise but you.
> Stranger: I wear no mask.
> Camilla: (Terrified, aside to Cassilda.) No mask? No mask!

The amoral civilisation trope – the 'evil elf' trope, if you will – comes to us like this visitor. Because what is this desire to create and read about not-quite-humans in fine apparel, who are simultaneously better and worse than us? It's an encounter with the self, a stranger self, both wicked and beautiful, like a glance into some stygian mirror with a gilt frame. I got that sensation writing *Pennyblade*, my most divisive novel, with its first-person view from the eyes of a she-elf whose moral landscape is an island to ours. The freedom from human concerns is a rather exhilarating state to write about, frankly, and the repulsion that follows quickly on exhilaration's heels reminds me I'm human, or thereabouts. I first felt that kick long ago, I've come to recall, when I first read *Elric of Melniboné*. A sort of othering of the self, a world both recognisable and alienating, horrific and comely. A mask that is a face.

Mythmaking and Tradition

Modern fantasy fiction rests upon a heritage as old as mankind itself. It's no coincidence that contemporary stories often rely on reworked versions of myths, legends and fairy tales, retelling the old stories in new ways – but while it is steeped in tradition, what we think of as *fantasy* is also constantly changing, finding new ways to express our fascination with the magical lure of imagined worlds.

The following essays consider just a few of the genre's conventions and subgenres, offering insight into the freedoms – and restraints – that come along with them. Whether you're interested in dragons and epic heroes, or writing children's books and working within existing franchises, these four authors shine a light on the paths you might want to take.

The Domestic and the Divine

Hannah Kaner

Where is adventure found? Traditions of fantasy, western fantasy in particular, balance their stories on the driving edge of a blade, in the hooves of the charging horse, the worn soles of walking boots and the weary back of the errant adventurer. The Hero's Journey, or the conceptual monomyth, we see over and over. Our stories are founded in the *Odyssey*, the *Mort-D'Arthur*, *Gawain and the Green Knight*, the *Faerie Queene*, the 'gentle knight... pricking on the plaine'.

Those they leave behind, the loss of the home they loved, are left to be the driving force of the individual's becoming, a springboard to the future, not the source of their power. We are convinced, as Ursula Le Guin critiques in her essay 'The Carrier Bag Theory of Fiction', that 'the proper shape of the narrative is that of the arrow or spear, starting *here* and going straight *there*', and we press these domestic quietudes into service of the hero. They become a raison d'etre, not a thing within themselves.

In *Godkiller*, I leaned into the Hero's Journey in all its glory, writing through it my love of classic fantasy, the quest, the fallen world, to find new magic and bring it home. My debut novel was, in essence, based on the 'there and back again', the call to adventure, the wandering warrior and the knight errant.

However, I also challenged it, breaking out of its trajectory. The role of adventurer-hero was fulfilled by a woman who just wants to sit at home, the secrets they uncover are not treasures of distant lands, but knowledge of the home they left behind. Essentially, the discovery the heroes must make is not out in the wilderness, but within themselves.

Godkiller is also an intentional play on the power of place. It pauses in quiet moments, around a campfire or in a new city. I oriented the world around gods born out of homes, rivers and wells, as well as war, industry and activity. I wanted to remind us where our stories come from, where we first exchanged them, sharing food around a fire, to while away the long hours of the night.

The Hero's Journey is a joyful and endless source of inspiration for fantasy novels. However, I want to encourage writers, and readers, to make room for the imaginative power, the fulcrum and potency, of the home. I want to explore connections between magic, divinity, and domesticity, and use these pages here to contrast the epic quest, to turn the hero back again.

The Power of the Home

The narrative tradition of the hearth is full of potential, and I encourage writers to not become too fixed on what fantasy should be, what adventure must be. To question its hyper-masculinised and hyper-westernised mythical threads. The home is a meeting point, a cooking pot, the point of exchange, the source of our safety, and a place of discovery. The home as not a trap, nor a service, but itself a source. Do not think your story is less a story if it does not contain new worlds and places, nor ourselves less writers because financially, physically or timewise we cannot take ourselves on quests and adventures. We do not need to go out to find gods and magic and inspiration, but we can go within.

Protection

Strength sometimes lies in the very fact of the four walls, manor or manger, of where we rest our heads, cook our food, rub our hands at the hearth. In Jessica John's brilliant novel *Bad Cree*, only by returning home does her protagonist begin to resolve the dangers in her dreams and the mystery of her sister's death. But her return comes with the fear of unravelling, the fear of welcoming danger in, of opening up grief and seeing it for all it is. Bringing a guest into the home holds the potential for opening the doors to treachery or change, but also opens the possibility of connection and community. Further, while some of the well-known gods of the western canon live at a distance, in the divine domesticity of Valhalla or Olympus, some still bury their roots in the household. In these roots, we find there is more to myth than quest, and more to divinity than lightning bolts and terror.

A favourite deity of mine is Brid of Ireland, associated with both the Tuatha Dé Danann and adapted into the Christian Saint Brigit, protector of the household. Known as the exalted one, Brid is one of the most celebrated descendants of the Tuatha Dé Danann. She is a symbol of the ending of winter, and her three-pointed crosses of straw are still hung from the rafters of Ireland to invoke blessings upon the house for the rest of the year. As the god and saint of poets, smiths, healing and protection, she is also the guardian of guest rights and the laws of hospitality.

Divinely protected rights of hospitality recur around the world. In Sanskrit, the saying 'Atithi Devo Bhava' means the guest is akin to god. Krishna in Hindu mythology sets the example of how guests should be greeted, in the Bhagavata-Purana washing the feet of an impoverished stranger. Household protection is upheld, too, by Hestia of Greece, Vesta of Rome or the cult of the Lares. These gods of the hearth are the guardians of Xenia, the laws of hospitality by which alliances are forged, or peace brokered. These laws of how guests should be treated, how peace and alliances should be forged, have long been essential to the safety of our communities.

However, when those laws are broken, the repercussions can be felt for generations. Think of House Atreus, which was destroyed through repeated violations of guest rights: fathers eating sons, parents slaughtering children, brothers destroying brothers. More recently, the Glencoe Massacre of 1692 was perpetrated by Clan Campbell, who violated the rules of hospitality and turned on their hosts. The clan was ostracised for centuries, and still pubs in Glencoe will have signs denying entry to Campbells. The household is to be protected, peace and balance maintained, and the consequences are dire.

The home has power. Monarchs are made and broken at the dining table, in bedchambers, at court, sometimes by their own children, their own guests. Tales of succession and inheritance begin in the bed, with favoured children or new-forged friendships changing balances of power. Bringing a guest into the home holds the potential to open doors to treachery or change, and the exchange of power or rise of rebellion can begin in the usurpation of household laws. In myth, Medea destroyed her home and family when it was disrespected by her husband; in history, Boudicca went to war over the violation of her rights, and her daughter's rights, of inheritance and succession.

The power here, of welcome and protection and guardianship, is a fascinating imaginative space. Perhaps the home is the space for adventurers to return to, but it is also the roof under which enemies or friends must break bread together under threat of the gods' anger.

Ancestry

The divinity of the household is not, then, just in the welcoming of guests and those outside, but guarding the potential contained within. The guardians of the home desire the power to defend against treachery and sickness; they desire safety for their children, their clan and vassals, and their future. They also want to guard the legacy of those who have come before.

Ancestry, the dubious potential of inheritance, and succession are fascinating aspects of domestic and divine life. Some communities in Africa, such as the Fang of Gabon, connect both ancestor and stranger with similar laws of hospitality, seeing a chance passerby as the potential embodiment of an ancestor who is owed welcome and warm treatment. Domestic practices in Korea and China include the ritual of honouring ancestors, a spiritual and powerful practice of finding those who came before as sources of wisdom, peace, and guidance. Legacy holds divine potential, and a strong connection from parent to child, aunt to niece, in a link of fealty and obligation which, in the Fang people, also extends to the welcome of a stranger.

Other cultures celebrate their ancestors in daily practices or national holidays. In southern Ethiopia, the Konso people pour beer onto the floor in ritual feasts to celebrate and feed their ancestors. Similarly, in Central America and Mexico, the Día de los Muertos sees *ofrendas* built with flowers and food, to guide family back to the home. Bringing it back around to gods, the rituals of libation appear in Incan culture and the Quechua, who also pour their drink or *chica* on the ground for the Pachamama, the Earth Mother, and – prior to August, their sowing season – families gather to cook for the Earth Mother all night to wish for plenty in the following year.

These connections with history, deep in the rituals of celebration, of domestic life, of gathering of their people, and the honouring of the dead are all sources of power. But they can be sources of danger too. What if the chance stranger becomes a terror? What if the ancestors have no good things to say? What if our inheritance threatens us? In her incredible book *Dazzling*, British-Nigerian writer Chikọdịlị Emelụmadụ writes of two girls, Treasure and Ozoemena. Ozoemena has inherited her family legacy of connection to the Igbo goddess Idemili and becomes a leopard. Treasure, however, has inherited a familial betrayal, and makes a deal with a spirit to bring her father back. Here, Emelụmadụ explores in the power of home and inheritance the dangers of legacy, and absence, a household upended, an inheritance refused.

As a writer, I would warn against lifting other cultures' stories, myths and practices and using them for your own devices, thus shedding them of context and power. However, I would recommend looking widely, reading deeply, and expanding or challenging your own expectations of what fantasy must be. What stories can we tell of divinity and domesticity? Of treachery and invasion? Of gods and broken laws, of hospitality and betrayal? Can we unlock the potency in this, bringing out the power of domestic life, real life, in the realm of fantasy and fae? The divinities of the house and home, family and inheritance are potent. Even if they lie in wait, they bear the weight of nations.

Danger

So there is danger, too, in the magic of the contained space. As we see in the broken laws of Xenia, household gods are not always benign. Perhaps they are tricksters, gods or angels seeing if your hospitality is truly up to scratch. Perhaps they are invaders, like Trow or Boggarts, come to warm themselves on your fire without your invitation, or curdle your milk if you don't keep them away with salt. Or they might begin as helpful, like Brownies or Duende, such as those appearing in Sam K. Horton's recent fantasy novel *Gorse*, but turn brutal with a simple slip, such as cutting off a toe while they try to trim your nails.

In previous essays in this series, authors have written about the Uncanny. This is a state which exists within the shroud of a familiar surface, if only you dare to peel back the layers. The home is not unthreatening; sometimes it is under threat, sometimes it is the threat itself.

Some of my favourite kinds of household stories are somewhere between fairy tale and folk horror. Dark with warning, they speak of a different kind of magic. They are gifts, cautions, an exchange of knowledge of what might go right in a home and what may go terribly wrong. For example, in Kirsty Logan's book of short stories *A Portable Shelter,* where two women tell tales to their unborn child, preparing them for the future, mixing love with fear and hope. In *House of Leaves* by Mark Z. Danielewski, a new home for a family quickly becomes a source of terror. Seeking the ambivalence of any concept, even one that is support to be protective or anchoring, such as the home, is a source of great stories.

In the *Godkiller* books, I wanted to lean into the ambivalence of the divine, for both protagonists and antagonists to occupy a space of opportunity, where they can turn or be turned for good and ill. Hseth was a god of the wildfires used to clear heather on mountains, but become a god of wealth and then war. Yusef is a god of safe haven, of finding home or the power of return, but by book three is reborn in a different shape, for the world has moved on from how he was originally imagined. The simplest, most platitudinous idea can become warped, sometimes cruel.

There is sometimes a desire in writing stories of heroism and action, fantasy and adventure, that danger must come from without. It must come from the invader, the great evil, the big bad, to be conquered, contained and subjected to the rule of the right. That there is indeed a right to be had, a simple conclusion, where good will win. I do love these stories, I love the hope and joy they bring. However, I love, too, the stories that turn inwards, those that do not hide our humanity from us: the stories of sharing, of exchange, of guardianship, but also cruelty, ambivalence, and danger. Essentially, I love stories of discovery.

Knowledge

Discovery is a driving aspect of the quest narrative and the assumption that *elsewhere* is the source of new knowledge. Gods above, magic abroad, secret worlds and high seas adventures. It is a commonly held belief that has also driven the exotification and commodification of other cultures, turning people into objects to be gawked over, their countries to be exploited, their wealth extracted and used for other means. Charlie English in *The Book Smugglers of Timbuktu* draws a distinct and direct line between the European cult of the adventurer in the eighteenth century and the propaganda and direction of colonisation on the African continent.

The home can be left out of such tales of discovery, the *here* to *there*. However, English also explores the work of Dr Abdel Kader Haidara, who preserved and smuggled texts out of threatened Timbuktu in 2012–13. Many of these extraordinary works had been under the guardianship of home librarians who had been inheriting their role and their texts for generations. Haidara's efforts were a direct inspiration for the work of the archivists in my own book, *Sunbringer*. Similarly, Arren's mapping of his own country has the caveated intent of domination and control. Again, I love adventure stories, but I am fascinated by their flaws, and their place in history.

What can one find at their own hearth, in their own hands? Malian scholars guarded generations of knowledge under their own roofs, and it is precisely in the home where some of the most extraordinary discoveries have taken place. Violet Moller writes in her history *Inside the Stargazer's Palace* that over the fourteenth to eighteenth centuries (emphasis mine):

> The stars, the weather, magic, geometry, tides, rhinoceroses, pigments, sacred languages, all were for the taking, all studied in the same place, a place that was often a hybrid museum, library, laboratory and observatory, from *inside the family home* – the natural world was investigated in kitchens, cellars, attics, bedrooms and garden sheds.

Deborah Harkness agrees that 'for a relatively brief time in the sixteenth and seventeenth centuries, the household bridged the gap between the monastery and the laboratory'. And here became a nexus between science and mysticism, alchemy and chemistry, astrology and astronomy, deduction and messages from the divine.

The distinctions we hold today have been split over time and experiment, but they were not always so. Most astronomers of the time supported their work through astrology and horoscopes, finding the future for kings, looking for messages from angels. This scrutiny of the world and the firmament were driving forces behind the improvement in accuracy, measurement, tools and diagrams. The search for the magic life-preserver, the philosopher's stone, which we still hold in our imaginative hearts, occurred in chemical exploration in basements and in kitchens, and drove scientific discovery towards pigments, mass glass production, and finer medicine. The source of revolution, the generation of space writing and our understanding of the magic of the stars above our heads and the dream for immortality thrived in copying, translating, working experimentally in the household.

This was often for safety as well as financial necessity. Regiomontanus was one of the first to retranslate and add to Ptolemy's *Almagast*, which had in turn been preserved and received contributions from Arabic and Hebraic study. A huge number of such texts were targeted and destroyed in religious backlash against Jewish and Muslim Europeans through purges such as the Spanish Inquisition. Previous such purges, and those that followed, also targeted works and contributions by women. When the books were burning, the few that survived were often preserved by people who took them inside their personal homes and libraries. They were not safe in places of public or dogmatic scrutiny, such as universities or monasteries.

However, because this work was done in the home, does not mean it was done alone. Here we can also banish from our imaginations the idea of a man, specifically, isolated in an ivory tower. One of the most famous of this era, Tycho Brahe, was assisted by his sister Sophia, who made discoveries of her own. Many of these philosophers not only knew of each other, and read each other's texts, but they occupied the same spaces. Johannes Kepler worked under Brahe, and his three laws defining planetary motion. Gerardus Mercator and Andreas Vesalius, who mapped the world and the human body respectively, were friends from university and spent many nights under the same roof. It is community and closeness that begets genius, not isolation; we seek those who share our values, challenge our assumptions, and break bread with them. This is where magic is found.

Elision

I have spent much of this essay celebrating the home, but I have touched on some of its challenges, too. These household laboratories could not have existed without the support and work of women who have been elided from history through religious pressure, financial restrictions and social mores. While the powerful gods of the hearth and home were earlier represented by women, I have to wonder if this is as much restriction as celebration? Are these women bound within their guarded spaces? Do we consider the chatelaine as precise an instrument as the star map? The kitchen as chemically explosive as the laboratory? The shield, or the pen for that matter, as powerful as the sword?

In her book *Small Fires*, Rebecca May Johnson feels that we are 'taught that the work of critical thinking takes place outside of the kitchen', that the 'domestic space is not connected to the endeavour of serious thought'.[1] She unpicks the assumption of the domestic space as a place of power, yes, but a place of gendered power. The goddesses I began with are not gods, they are protectors, not rulers. Hestia is a child of Zeus, Brigid of Dagda. These are guards, not knights errant. It is something that comes up over and over again, for me personally, for writers, for women. Is the domestic space by definition feminine, and is the feminine, by tradition, circumscribed?

This leads me back to traditions of western fantasy and myth, and my own frustrations with this feminine-domestic-enclosed thought line that encouraged me to write my own wandering warrior as a woman. A woman unafraid, unashamed and unthreatened by her femininity. We want to read and write worlds where women are warriors too, where the wild is claimed and tamed, where we can wield our own swords. Importantly, where we can camp under the stars without the fear of bears or men, or gods. This is inspiration too, to break from tradition, to challenge its expectations

However, I wish to be wary of dismissing the power of the home, the hearth, hospitality, the poets and protection even in

---

1   Johnson, Rebecca May, *Small Fires* (Pushkin, 2022) p. 12.

the moments I break out of it. Who am I to scorn Penelope, with her wily weaving, who kept guard over Ithica? Who would I be to dismiss Hild, the adviser of kings and bishop-maker and monastic founder in Northumbria? Can we find power in domestic spaces that escapes the expectations that the space must be hyper-feminised or restrictive, or both?

* * *

I have primarily used the concept of the domestic and the divine here to contrast the Hero's Journey. I wanted to pull out the threads of fantasy, magic and adventure that can be tied to going *within*, rather than *without*. There are so many more threads to pull: the home as a portal, the home as a character in the Gothic, the home as a shrine, the home as a spaceship, the home as a cave, the home as eldritch terror. The home is not the antithesis to adventure, nor adventure the antithesis to the home. If I want you to take anything from this essay, it's to challenge the assumptions you may have over what fantasy can and should be, over what you're permitted to write.

We began here with the gods of the home and hearth, but I think we have seen too that we cannot draw a wall between divinity and fae, spirit and ancestor, house and adventure. Must we? When writing fantasy the possibilities are limitless, the opportunities as unending as your own imagination. Look inside, to the things you love about the stories you know, challenge what you don't, and go deeper and deeper, wider and wider, until you find new wellsprings of inspiration – as

Emelụmadụ says in *Writing the Uncanny*, 'The entire world is your buffet. And use a ladle would you? The good stuff is at the bottom of the pot.'

I would build on this, and say: go into the back of your own cupboards, go into the dark spaces of history, go into the ashes of the hearth. Dig deep, and pull magic from the dust.

On the Nature of Dragons

Charlotte Bond

When I got my author copies of *The Fireborne Blade* from my publisher, my daughter asked if she could read one. She was excited because, previously, I'd mostly written horror and she wasn't allowed to read that.

I didn't need to seek out her feedback, because later that same day she came up to me and said, 'I've read the beginning and I have some thoughts.'

'Oh, yes,' I replied, somewhat dubiously. I'm a freelance editor by day, and I could tell from her tone that she'd listened to me talk critically about books more than I'd previously thought.

'It was good, Mum, but you didn't really describe the dragon in the first chapter. I couldn't visualise it very well.'

When I looked back, she was correct: I'd spent virtually no time describing the dragon. It made me question myself: had I done something wrong? On reflection, no. I didn't go into detail because the opening chapter is not the start of the character's narrative but an excerpt from a book that exists within the Fireborne world called *The Demise and Demesne of Dragons*. This fictional tome is a record of all the various encounters between knights and dragons (which frequently do not end well). The opening chapter is a statement given by a knight to the mages who record all such details. So, of course it was natural that he wouldn't describe the dragon. In my world, dragons are common, and each dragon has a special human name. In chapter one, it's the Glebe-Reaver being described, and anyone reading the book in-world will know what the Glebe-Reaver looks like (or will, at least, know where else in *The Demise and Demesne of Dragons* they can find a description). To describe the dragon in detail would be nonsensical from the world's point of view.

Describing something already known to characters has been called by various names: info dump, exposition, or 'As you know'. It's when a character states something that is blindingly obvious to everyone around them because it's necessary for the reader or viewer to have this information to hand. I wanted to avoid that, so I took a bit of a shortcut and went with the theory that if I say 'dragon' then everyone is pretty much going to imagine something similar.

Reader assumptions about dragons is the place where all writers should start. They should ask themselves: what do people already know or assume about dragons? And which of those assumptions do I want to keep or discard?

Non-fiction Research

To decide what to include or exclude, a writer has to examine what has gone before. What have other writers done? What are the real-life legends about dragons that can be drawn on or turned on their head?

When researching for *The Fireborne Blade*, I borrowed an amazing book from the library (if you're a writer, your local library is invaluable in so many ways) called *British Dragons* by Jacqueline Simpson. With individual chapters devoted to the habits and habitats of dragons, the hero, and the tactics of dragoncide, it provided little snippets of information that filtered their way into the book. It's a great resource for those who want to ground their dragons in the legends that already exist.

There are plenty of dragon legends that a reader can exploit. For example, a favourite of mine ever since I read Usborne's *Mysteries of the Unknown* (familiar to so many of my generation) was The Lambton Worm. This dragon was featured in book one of *Mysteries of the Unknown* and the illustration was particularly graphic. The Lambton Worm was caught by John Lambton when fishing in the River Weir. Revolted by his catch, he discarded it and threw it into a well. There, the worm thrived and grew, crawling out to terrorise beasts and humans. Plenty of people tried to kill it, but every time it was sliced apart, the separate parts fitted themselves back together again.

In the end, John Lambton returned and was forced to deal with the monster. After consulting a witch, he covered his armour in long, sharp spikes. He then engaged the worm in battle but made sure to do it in the middle of the river – that way, when the worm was sliced apart by his armour, the parts would float off down the river before they could join up again.

This story made such an impact on me that when I wrote *The Bloodless Princes*, I used elements of it in a creation myth. But while *Mysteries of the Unknown* was crucial in sparking my interest, it was to Simpson's *British Dragons* that I turned to ensure the accuracy of the story.

Another invaluable book is *The Penguin Book of Dragons*. Several historical details from this book made their way into my fiction, such as the idea that a dragon's brain becomes a precious stone after it dies, a stone known as *draconitis* or *draconita*. In some legends, this stone can only be obtained from the brain of a living dragon, so magicians would have to find ways to cut it out of a sleeping dragon – which sounds like a short story all by itself! Robin McKinley used a dragonstone as a plot point in her book *The Hero and the Crown*, and I also used it in *The Bloodless Princes*.

Another interesting fact from history was that Pliny the Elder, in his book *Natural History*, stated that the natural enemy of dragons was elephants. According to *The Penguin Book of Dragons*, a dragon would wrap its coils around an elephant to kill it, but then the weight of the dying elephant as it fell to the ground would crush the dragon and ultimately kill it as well. Think of all the books where the hero starts out finding a dragon's egg – how much more inventive if they found a dying dragon half-crushed under a dead elephant?

However, what was really interesting to me was the fact that once Pliny had written this, the detail filtered its way into other texts, such as those by medieval monks, and Lucan's poem *Pharsalia*. Medieval Christian thinkers even suggested that there might be an allegory for Adam and Eve in there. In 1030, a monk named Arnold wrote about the time he encountered a dragon, and a footnote in *The Penguin Book of Dragons* notes that he seems to be quoting verbatim a chapter from Isidore's *Etymologies*. This is just a shortened list of examples – find the book and look for all mentions of elephants and you'll find plenty more.

It astonished me that one comment about dragons versus elephants had made it into history as fact. In tribute to this, elephants made a brief appearance in *The Bloodless Princes*, but the idea that a single comment could filter through so many sources as fact actually led me to explore, in book two, how stories are told and believed. In *The Bloodless Princes*, the cut-away sections are no longer just from *The Demise and Demesne of Dragons* but come from other in-world sources – including the stories told by the dragons themselves, as I explored how facts can get repeated, twisted, or misinterpreted, depending on the audience. When that happens, how do we sort truth from fiction and heroes from villains?

Incidentally, if you're looking for nemeses for your dragon, don't neglect the humble panther. Both *The Penguin Book of Dragons* and other sources (such as the Getty blog)[1] note that in the medieval bestiary, the panther was often associated with Christ because legend has it that after it had eaten, it would sleep in a cave for three days. Its breath smells of allspice and all animals will follow its sweetness – except dragons. Dragons are beasts that belong to the Devil, so it's natural that they

1   blogs.getty.edu/iris/the-panther-alpha-and-omega-of-the-medieval-bestiary/

would not be drawn by the sweetness of the panther. Thus, in the age-old battle of Christians against the Devil, we now have dragon versus panther.

When searching for inspiration, don't be reticent about looking at children's factual books. While the Penguin and Simpson books were amazing resources, I also got a few ideas from books such as *Demons and Dragons* by Alice Peebles, *Dragons* by John Malam and *Dragons* by Charlotte Guillain. Such books can be invaluable, not only because they have amazing illustrations that might fire a spark in your imagination, but because sometimes truth and facts can be distilled down and presented to children in a simplistic way that sheds a whole new light on the subject.

For example, Malam's book has a different legend on each page, with stories from Denmark (Beowulf), Scandinavia and Germany (Fafnir and Sigurd), Switzerland (Stempflin and the dragon), Iraq (Tiamat), Turkey and Libya (St George), China (the pearl and the Queen Mother), Japan (How the Jellyfish Lost Its Bones), and India (Vritra). It, too, alludes to the existence of a dragonstone.

Peebles's book lists ten beasts from mythology and gives them 'Beast Power' ratings in categories such as Strength, Ferocity, and Repulsiveness. Among the ten beasts are The Lindwurm, Fafnir, the Firedrake, the Seven-headed Dragon, Echidna, and Illuyanka. In the same way that there are hierarchies in nature, so there should be in dragons too – but what would make a dragon feared by humans or other dragons? That's fertile ground for the writer's imagination. There were also other mythical creatures in this book, such as the Chimera, the Oni, and the Furies. This can help the aspiring writer populate their world with other beasts, because if dragons exist, what else might there be?

I will admit that the pictures in this book are pretty appalling, a mishmash of cut-and-paste elements that do not blend well, but I did like how each beast had a section entitled 'How to defeat', which would provide some interesting ideas for writers. For example, to chase away an Oni, you throw peaches at it, since the fruit was believed to have power over evil spirits. However, beans or sardine heads will also work. That's the kind of detail that you just can't make up as a writer: defeat by peaches.

For inspiration, we can't forget that the huge, sprawling world of D&D can now provide authors with ideas as to what their dragons might look like and what characteristics they might have. For my part, I kept away from D&D because I was worried that some of my dragons might end up looking a bit too similar to a D&D dragon, which leads to a whole wealth of copyright issues. Instead, I turned to books like *Dracopedia Field Guide* by William O'Connor. The illustrations are gorgeous, and I used them as a starting point to create my own race of creatures. *Dracopedia* also gave me the idea of how my dragons evolved and interbred with other animals (more on that below).

Fiction: What Has Gone Before

Dragons have popped up time and again in fantasy literature and movies, featuring as main characters, foes, and sidekicks.

Like so much in fantasy, the work of J.R.R. Tolkien holds a huge amount of influence here. Smaug in *The Hobbit* is perhaps the epitome of fantasy dragons.

If I felt bad about not describing the look of a dragon in my first book, then I found myself in good company with Tolkien. Smaug is mentioned by Thorin in chapter one of *The Hobbit*, but rather than describing what he looks like, Thorin talks about the nature of dragons in general: they steal gold and jewels then guard them; they live practically forever; they can't make anything for themselves, not even mending their own scales; and when it comes to treasure, 'they hardly know a good bit of work from a bad, though they usually have a good notion of the current market value.'

We finally get to see him in chapter twelve, where he is described as a vast red-gold dragon with a coiled tail and bat-like wings. He has wisps of smoke coming from his nose and jaws, and his body is crusted with gems from lying on his hoard for so long. All in all, pretty close to the archetypal dragon that we'd expect. He turns out to be cunning, greedy, and destructive.

In the 1960s, Anne McCaffery caught the literary imagination with her Dragonriders of Pern series, where the dragons were more like sentient horses. These dragons didn't guard gold but kept the kingdom safe from Threads. I was surprised to read on the blurb that this was strictly classed as a science-fiction novel, but there are plenty of elements here to justify such categorisation, since the action is set on a distant planet and the threat of the Threads from the Red Sun definitely have a sci-fi feel to them. While McCaffery's dragons appear like fantasy beasts in most respects, their eyes are more like insect eyes than mammalian or reptile, and they fly in the Between to get them places fast.

In *The Hero and the Crown* by Robin McKinley (1984), we have again the enduring idea of dragons as being beasts that ravage kingdoms. But McKinley challenged the idea that those hunting down dragons had to be bold, brave knights. Instead, her dragon-hunter is a young princess, Aerin. Now, it's not the knight saving the princess from the dragon but the princess saving the kingdom, which is a fantastic twist. I really loved how there weren't only big, terrifying dragons in the kingdom but also little dragons that were destructive and seen as vermin.

When it came to my own books, I chose a similar path to *The Hero and the Crown* in that my protagonist, Maddileh, is female. However, rather than being a princess out to prove herself, she's a simple baron's daughter who becomes a knight. For me, exploring the world around dragon-hunting (which I imagined as some kind of boys' club) was as important to me as detailing the individual quest.

Guards! Guards! by Terry Pratchett (1989) continues with the idea of male heroes fighting hungry dragons that hoard gold and prey on princesses. But this is Pratchett, so his male heroes are not knights but policemen, the princess is a rather rotund woman who has more gumption than any of the men around her, and while there is a single 'noble' dragon, we also have swamp dragons – my favourite addition to the dragon menagerie. Swamp dragons are not magical; they've just evolved from larger dragons and are only dangerous because they sometimes accidentally blow themselves up. Their ability to breathe fire isn't magical but organic, with the flames being created by internal organs that produce flammable gas. But that makes their stomachs incredibly unstable, so that they're prone to exploding at even the slightest bit of indigestion. They are not aggressive but kind of cute and squeaky. They don't hunt sheep or cattle but eat coal, and they're not interested in gold, much preferring a scratch behind the ears from a brave human. These swamp dragons are ingenious fictional beasts, and it's clear that Pratchett has really sat down and thought about exactly how an animal that breathes fire would exist in the world.

The Temeraire series by Naomi Novik, which started with *His Majesty's Dragon* (also known as *Temeraire* in the UK) in 2006, posits a world where dragons existed in the nineteenth century and thus are used as war steeds in the Napoleonic Wars. If you take a step back from book one and look at it critically, you'll see that not very much happens. Contrast it to McCaffery's *Dragonflight*, where there's danger and drama every few chapters. But the delight of Novik's book is that it focuses on the relationship between dragon and rider. It's a slow burn but I loved how she really went into the minutiae of dragon care and what that bond would mean for both dragon and human.

In the world of *The Mountain Crown* by Karin Lowachee, people are sent to capture dragons in the same way that a farmer might cull deer on his land. Capturing and removing the dragons from the wild is a way of ensuring the wild dragons don't get unruly and wreak havoc on human habitations. Only the Ba'Suon tribe are able to do this, due to the deep and unique connection they have with dragons that enables cross-species communication. But some of the dragons who are captured are used in fighting rings or controlled and manipulated into something akin to guard dogs. Here, the dragons are used to highlight issues around conquest, culture, and the exploitation of natural resources and living creatures.

The Executioner's Blade by Andrew Knighton (2024) doesn't have dragons as a main plot point, but they are woven into the world in a manner that makes them just as normal as dogs and cats but without losing their fantastical elements. I liked how they were particularly normalised as just part of the world.

No writer can read all the comparison dragons book out there before they start work, and *The Priory of the Orange Tree* by Samantha Shannon, *Sorcerer to the Crown* by Zen Cho, and *The Shadow of the Gods* by John Gwynne are some of the more popular books that I didn't get a chance to read before I started my own work. But if you're going to write your own dragons, it's highly advisable to read as many dragon books as you can to see what has gone before.

Dragons have always been popular with younger readers, and quite frequently those books make it onto the big screen, giving readers a chance to see these glorious beasts brought to life.

Eragon by Christopher Paolini (2002) seems to be hugely popular with teens, although I can't fathom why. The ideas in the book felt dull and the narrative came across as clunky. Still, it was hugely popular, and it once again tapped into the idea of dragons being steeds but with a special bond with their riders. The film, apparently, was even more disappointing than the book, and after a brief viewing of the beginning, I felt inclined to agree.

The book *How to Train Your Dragon* by Cornelia Funke, published 2003, had a more slapstick take on the idea of dragon riders, with her main character being called Hiccup Horrendous Haddock the Third. The plot starts out with Hiccup needing to capture a dragon to train as a right of passage. In a derivation from this idea, the 2010 film adaptation of the book had dragons and Vikings as enemies, and Hiccup had to convince the tough Vikings that dragons really weren't that bad. Personally, I much prefer the films.

Although many people dislike it, I feel that the 1996 film *Dragonheart*, directed by Rob Cohen, written by Charles Edward Pogue based on a story he wrote with Patrick Read Johnson, is a really interesting addition to dragon fiction. There is a bond between Draco and Bowen, but it's one that has to be earned, unlike other dragon fiction where a bond is formed much like a baby chick hatching to find its mother. In fact, Draco is more closely bonded to Einon, but that bond is actually sickening the kingdom and needs to be destroyed rather than nurtured. What I particularly liked about this film was how Draco was clearly intelligent and gruff and was just trying to make his way in the world like any other creature.

Another 'enemies to allies' film is *Damsel* (2024) starring Milly Bobby Brown. It was a nice idea and looked stunning, but I didn't find anything particularly new in it. However, Shohreh Aghdashloo's voicing of the dragon was a mesmeric performance.

Having read a decent number of books and watched the movies, I felt I was ready to consider just how I was going to make my own unique breed of dragons.

A Dragon's Appearance

Common dragon traits include the following: large wings; four limbs with the front two acting like arms; a snout; scales; the ability to breathe fire; and a distinctive colour. But there are, in fact, plenty of other types of dragons out there, and writers would be wise to diversify if they want their dragons to stand out.

So many of the fictional dragons featured in my list above would be categorised as a standard Western dragon. But there are African dragons and Chinese dragons as well, which might give a writer a whole new approach to their worldbuilding. A standard Western dragon has four limbs, two wings, scales, and a tail. Chinese dragons are often more serpentine and lack wings. Within African mythology, we can find rainbow serpents such as Aido-Hwedo and Denwen, a serpent made entirely of fire. There's the Ancient Greek monster, the hydra: a serpent in possession of many heads. Each time a head was cut off, another two would grow in its place.

Then there are creatures like wyverns, that have only a pair of back legs because their wings are pretty much where their front arms/legs/limbs would be. A wyrm traditionally has no wings and usually no legs either. Cockatrices and basilisks have also sometimes been included under the term 'dragon', yet you rarely see them in dragon fiction.

Size is something that needs to be considered carefully when it comes to a case of aerodynamics. Unless your dragon uses magic to fly, then their wings need to be large enough to lift their body off the ground. If you have a huge dragon, then it's going to need huge wings as well. Take a look at red kites or golden eagles by way of example.

According to the British Bird of Prey Centre, a red kite's body is 60–70cm long and its wingspan is 175–195cm.[2] This means its wings are roughly three times as long as its body. Translate this into a dragon, and however big your dragon is, its wingspan is going to be around three times that. If you imagine a dragon to be the size and length of a double-decker bus, then when unfurled, its wings will be two or three buses long. If you have your dragon wandering around a palace with its rider, or flying round its cave, then you need to think *really* big to ensure the space can accommodate such measurements.

Where is its Niche?

Perhaps the next biggest thing to consider after you've decided what your dragon looks like is where it sits in the world you have created. For this, you really need to consider things like: what do they eat? Where do they live? Are they solitary or gregarious? Did they evolve or were they created?

What they eat is quite challenging. A dragon is going to be an apex predator: top of the food chain. That's going to present problems for the rest of your fictional world.

---

2   www.britishbirdofpreycentre.co.uk/our-birds/red-kite/

In the real world, according to the International Wolf Center, wolves can survive on 2.5–3.7lb of meat daily, but a good diet to help them reproduce would be 5–7lb every day.[3] However, wolves typically have feast-or-famine lifestyles, meaning they can eat as much as 20lb of food in a single sitting. A grey wolf's weight can be between 31–143lb, with an average of 100lb.[4]

Now, let's scale it up for dragons. If your dragon weighed around 10,000lb, or 5 tons, then, scaling that up, you'd need about 250–370lb of meat a day, with a dragon being able to eat around 2,000lb of food in a single sitting. If a sheep weighs 80–100lb,[5] then a dragon needs 2–4 sheep a day, or can eat around 20 sheep in a single sitting. And that's just one dragon – a whole gang of them could seriously impact on local animal husbandry. Whether you choose to set your dragon story in a countryside populated by farmers or in an urban setting where your go-to is butchers to feed your military/royal dragons, then you're going to need to think about where that meat comes from.

Previous writers have tackled the problem in various ways. I particularly like Novik's solution, where a growing Temeraire has to go out and hunt fish to keep him fed while he's on the ship transporting him to land. Then they seem to have areas in the military training centre where they breed animals specifically to feed the dragons, something you also see in *Dragon-*

---

3   wolf.org/wolf-info/basic-wolf-info/biology-and-behavior/hunting-feeding-behavior/hungry-as-a-wolf-what-wolves-eat/

4   www.britannica.com/animal/gray-wolf

5   www.britannica.com/animal/domesticated-sheep

flight. I thought *Eragon* was a bit of a cop-out with its explanation that a 'sedentary' dragon doesn't eat very much at all, but one on the move in mating season needs to eat every week.

I quite liked Andrew Knighton's solution in his book *The Executioner's Blade*, where we see the local headsman delivering an executed body to a mountaintop where a wyvern stands ready to eat it. In that world, wyverns and other creatures consume the bodies of the dead, and rather than seeing this as sacrilege, humans have adapted so that leaving dead bodies exposed is part of the funeral ritual. The wyverns have found a niche among humans to exploit, and the humans have adapted.

My solution to the food problem? I cheated a little. My smaller dragons eat meat, but the really large ones are magical and they can be nourished by words. Much less taxing on the arable countryside. Another vegetarian-friendly option was provided by Terry Pratchett in his Discworld series, where the little swamp dragons are fed on coal. Of course, when a larger 'noble' dragon comes on the scene, we discover that its taste tends towards virginal human flesh. But there's only one noble dragon and many, many swamp dragons in the city, so the swamp dragons have found a more sustainable and urban solution that allows them to live alongside humans.

Obviously, if your dragons live in communities, the impact on the local sheep and cattle population is going to be more drastic. But as well as thinking about food sources, you have to ask yourself: why do they live in communities? Is it for protection? That seems unlikely, because they would surely be the apex predator in the land – unless there is some devastating weapon or extermination method that humans use, causing the dragons to band together for safety. Maybe they're social animals, like guinea pigs, that get lonely and pine if they live alone. Or maybe, if we go back to our earlier example, they're like wolves. While lots of fiction categorises wolves either as dangerous, lone predators or ruthlessly efficient pack-hunters, the reality is that they are highly social creatures that look after the sick and injured.[6] We might refer to a group of wolves as a 'pack', but really they're a community where pups are raised by many, the vulnerable are protected, and knowledge is passed down through the generations.

A Community of Dragons

In fiction, dragons are often portrayed as vicious and powerful, but if they live together, perhaps caring for the sick and the young, that opens up opportunities for writers to have more nuanced creatures in their stories rather than the traditional angry, greedy dragons we know. It also provides a new slant to relationships that goes beyond the traditional dragon and dragon-rider bond.

Thinking about how your dragons interact with the other animals in the world will help you decide on their ecological niche. It was while I was pondering this question for *The Fireborne Blade* that I realised some smaller, less magical dragons had, in the past, bred with other animals within the world. That's why some of my dragons had a cat-like appearance or

---

6   www.livingwithwolves.org/social-wolf-psa/

feathers. While this was my own idea, I can honestly say that I was influenced by the fabulous illustrations in *Dracopedia*, which made me think about how dragons might look like birds or eels.

Dragons and Humans

How dragons interact with humans (or, at least, main characters in humanoid form) is going to be a key part of any fantasy story. Are they going to be a mighty beast that needs to be vanquished? Or will there be a deep bond between one human and one dragon?

The human–dragon bond is a very well-used trope. In *When the Moon Hatched* by Sarah A. Parker, the dragons have such a special bond with humans they can die with you or for you. In *Dragonflight*, we are shown how devastating it can be for a dragon rider to lose his dragon, how it impacts every part of his life. In the film version of *How to Train Your Dragon*, it's the bond between Hiccup and Toothless that ends up changing attitudes on both sides of the species barrier. And in George R.R. Martin's A Song of Ice and Fire series, the bond between Daenerys and her dragons makes her a powerful leader – although only after she's had to birth them in fire and protect them as newly hatched babies, offering them protection that they later return. In many cases of a dragon-human bond, the human has to show good qualities before they are deemed worthy of a dragon bond. As noted above, the need to sever the dragon–human bond to save the kingdom was an interesting twist taken by the film *Dragonheart*, which is something that isn't explored much in fiction.

If the dragons are there to be conquered, then you need to give them a weakness. There's a wonderful exchange in Terry Pratchett's *Guards! Guards!* in which Carrot, Nobby, and Colon all discuss a dragon's 'voonerable spot', which is clearly a reference to *The Hobbit* and the fact that Smaug is finally conquered due to a *vulnerable* spot on his body where a scale had previously been knocked loose. Through this gap, the black arrow pierces Smaug's flesh and kills him.

With the old adage that a hero is only as heroic as their nemesis is evil, a character who can conquer and kill a mighty dragon is going to be a mighty hero. But given a dragon's size and advantages (such as claws and breathing fire), the hero might need help. In my Fireborne world, magical armour and weapons exist to try and counteract not just the might of the dragons hunted but also their own innate magic. In *The Hero and the Crown*, Aerin discovers a recipe for kennet, an ointment that can be rubbed on humans and horses to make them resistant to dragon fire. As McKinley so wryly observes in her narrative, if you're close enough to use a sword then you're close enough to be badly burned, so the kennet evens the balance a little. As it happens, this doesn't work against the great dragon Maur, but it works enough with the smaller dragons that Aerin can gain sufficient experience of fighting lesser dragons to help her defeat Maur when the time comes.

Of course, one of the main weaknesses for dragons in many books is humanity. Either we kill them, or subjugate them, or we win them over. In *The Mountain Crown*, even though the dragons are mighty, fire-breathing beasts, humanity captures them from the wild and uses them for (among other things) cage fights.

In the first book in my Fireborne series, I explored the world of knights hunting dragons. The favoured course of extermination is for a knight to find a dragon in its cave and slaughter it there (because it's impossible to kill them while airborne). I implemented three key hindrances to killing a dragon. Firstly, their skin is pretty tough – not impenetrable, but magic weapons are required to pierce it. Secondly, their magic leaks into the tunnels around their caves, meaning that you might get killed by dragon-dead or other nasty things before you even get in sight of the dragon. And thirdly, killing a dragon will unleash the magic within it, often in a very violent or destructive way. One dragon blows up; the flesh of another dragon liquifies into sentient sludge with a fierce hunger for flesh. Killing a dragon, in my world, is something undertaken by either the brave or the reckless.

Returning to the maxim that the hero's victory is only as glorious as his opponent's evil, an intelligent dragon is going to pose more of a threat than one that is nothing better than an animal. If it doesn't have that, then your story is basically going to be humans hunting a big, dumb beast, which is no story at all.

The Knotty Question of Speech

Humans consider speech a sign of intelligence, and for a writer it's also a handy way for your human protagonists to communicate with the dragons. If your dragon is to pose a threat, then it can speak calumnies and curses; if your dragon is going to be a helper character, then it can offer advice to the other characters. Crucially, if there is going to be a bond, then there must be some form of communication so that mutual trust and respect can be formed.

When it comes to communication, careful thought must be given as to how this will take place. In *The Hobbit*, we are merely told that Smaug speaks and the reader is left to imagine that. But in *The Hobbit: The Desolation of Smaug* (2013), we see that the dragon speaks like anyone else – by moving his lips into recognisable shapes that match the words he is speaking. The same is true of *Dragonheart*. After watching both those movies, I have to say that I chose to go with telepathy because the lips of a giant lizard moving to human speech just looked weird. (Interestingly, the lips of the dragon in *Damsel* also move when she speaks, but not in a way that seems to correspond with the sounds being made. The lips just move up and down, which is even worse that lizard lips moving like human lips.)

In Novik's books, Temeraire the dragon also speaks so that everyone can hear him. In contrast, the dragons in *Dragonflight*, *The Mountain Crown*, *The Hero and the Crown*, and *Eragon* all communicate telepathically.

Somewhat uniquely, in Cornelia Funke's books, the dragons speak 'Dragonese', which has phrases like 'me like' for 'I like you' and 'yum-yum' for 'bite'.[7] In contrast, in the movie versions of *How to Train Your Dragon*, Toothless manages to communicate with Hiccup through body language and facial expressions. The

7   howtotrainyourdragon.fandom.com/wiki/Dragonese

appearance and personality of Toothless was modelled on cats, dogs, and horses, and that can be seen quite clearly in some of the actions that Toothless takes and how Hiccup interprets them. Body language is an equally valid, more subtle, and – in the film's instance – more comedic method of communication. It is perhaps harder to put forward in a book, where words are needed to describe every muscle twitch and eye movement, but it can be done. In fact, to my mind, it can be an even more poignant way for two characters to communicate.

Apart from Funke's books, where there is a specific dragon language, all of the dragons who speak to humans seem to speak English. Perhaps a writer should ask: why is that? Or is it the case that we're all speaking dragon? For my part, I decided that my dragons would speak in kennings: compound terms that replace a single noun. They are prevalent in *Beowulf*, with my favourite example being 'heather-stepper' for a deer, which made it into *The Bloodless Princes*. But I mostly invented my kennings to be specific to dragons, such as 'ground-skitters' for mice, 'deep-dwellers' for dragons, and my personal favourite, 'ground-clouds' for sheep. Writing a whole new language for my dragons made their culture and their intelligence come alive for me, proving that examining the issue of language can take your dragons and your world in a whole new direction.

Gold, Gold, Gold

One question you will have to address is: do my dragons love gold? And if so, why? If you decide that gold is merely a meaningless base metal and your dragons are far too intelligent to care about such shininess, then you need to think about what they *do* care about.

If you decide to stick with tradition and your dragons are going to be the usual types of hoarders, then you need to ask yourself why. In the past, it was fine to just say that dragons loved gold, but that's not really the case anymore. People want characters in the books they're reading to be well-rounded and relatable. I particularly liked how, in Novik's books, riders would buy their dragon steeds little trinkets to cheer them up or win their loyalty. A hugely heartwarming aspect to William Laurence was just how much care and attention he put into buying Temeraire a golden chain, and I loved Temeraire's response when he received it.

When writing *The Fireborne Blade*, I was certainly going for the traditional in a big way, but that was because I wanted to subvert the trope of a male knight going on a dragon hunt by making that knight female. So, my dragons had to love gold – which they did, but a little like Tolkien, my dragons had no sense of worth. A tin bath or a shiny mirror, some roof tiles or a metal teapot were hoarded alongside gems and precious metals.

Then, in book two, the reader comes to learn exactly why the dragons love gold, silver, and gems so much. The book is peppered with dragon mythology alongside human mythology, and the dragon creation myth states that dragons had the world first and humans encroached on that. But, being noble creatures, they agree with their god's plea to share this fertile world. When it becomes clear that the humans are multiplying faster

than the dragons and need a lot more of the earth for cultivating their crops, the god asks the dragons to go live under the
earth. To make their new home more inviting, the god fills it
with 'earth-ribbons' and 'stone-eyes' (my kennings for precious
metals and gems), and the dragons are well-pleased with their
sparkling new home.

However, the humans see these shining caves and they want
a piece of it too, so they keep mining the gold and stealing
the gems. Consequently, when a dragon steals treasure from
a human, it's not a magpie-like hoarding instinct – it's simply
taking back what was already stolen.

Culture and Magic

If you make your dragons intelligent and able to speak, then you
hit upon an extra layer you need to interweave into your narrative: culture. This is touched upon a little bit in the film *Dragonheart*, where Draco looks up at the sky and talks to Bowen about
how the dragons have different names for the stars. This inspired
me to create my own culture for the dragons of the Fireborne
world, because if dragons can talk, then they can tell stories, and
sing. What would those stories look like? Who would the dragons hold up as heroes and villains? If they believe in an afterlife,
what does it look like? Who are their gods? If you want to go
down the route of making your dragons intelligent and able to
communicate, then you need to create a society for them as well.

Another element that writers need to consider is magic,
since dragons are inherently magical creatures. After all, while

dragons are flesh-and-blood creatures that breed, and eat, and fly, and can be killed in some way, the ability to fly such a great bulk around and breathe fire has to have some element of magic to it to make such impossible things achievable.

But while magic is an integral part of the dragon mythos, as writers we have to be wary of magic. It needs to be tightly controlled. After all, once you've got a giant lizard that can fly, breathe fire, and rend you limb from limb with its claws, that's kind of enough for a hero to go up against. If you make them masters of magic as well, then how is your hero going to defeat them?

With that in mind, the magical elements of dragons are often downplayed in books such as *The Mountain Crown* and *The Hobbit*, and films like *How to Train Your Dragon*, where the only thing magical is the fact that these great scaly beasts can fly and breathe fire. 'Minimal magic' dragons, if you will.

But dragons can have some magical elements, so long as they are limited. In Chinese and Japanese folklore, some dragons can manipulate the weather. In D&D, there are dragons that can cast spells. Some dragons have the capacity to become invisible.

In *The Hero and the Crown*, Maur's skull has a magical ability to pollute the world around it once it's hung up in the king's hall. It's only Aerin's insistence that it's moved to somewhere more remote – and, later, removed entirely – that reduces its corrupting influence. Recognising and overcoming that magic is a key part of Aerin's journey to her destiny. In my books, the noble dragons have magical abilities, but they've mostly been killed by the humans, so although the possibility is there (and is shown with The White Lady in book two), it's not front and centre. But certainly, magical dragons are not as frequently used by writers as the traditional flying dragon.

If the main point of your dragon is to be a foe, then you need to pick magical abilities that make them a more cunning combatant for your hero to defeat. A dragon that can turn invisible or one that can summon up a hurricane are going to be pretty formidable foes.

But if you want your dragon to have magic that is helpful, then, like all magical rules, you need to make sure that the magic isn't just a first resource for the characters. After all, if you had a tame dragon who could speak magic healing spells, where's the danger and drama in any battle? It's different if your character needs to win the dragon's trust first and earn the right to the spell, especially if that character needs to overcome centuries of human persecution of dragons.

Alternatively, the cost of magic can be high for the dragon. In *Dragonheart*, Draco has the power to give life to a human – but only if he gives away half his own heart. Even then, that magic is what turns Bowen against all dragons, because Bowen believes that this magic has actually poisoned his prince even as it saved him. In this way, writers Charles Edward Pogue and Patrick Read Johnson have not only limited the dragon's power, but have provided conflict and motive for the various characters.

* * *

A writer who thinks that throwing a dragon into the mix will help up the magical stakes without thinking through the ramifications of such a huge, imposing beast on the ecology and culture of the world they're creating is making a big mistake. A unicorn is just a type of horse; a harpy could easily occupy the niche of any carrion bird. But a dragon needs careful thought, and there's a wealth of prior dragon novels that show how it can be done well. That said, the time spent planning how to fit a dragon into your world might lead you in different directions that not only help your dragon fit into your world, but also take other aspects of your novel down unexpected and rewarding paths.

Vicarious Dreams:
Fantasy and Tie-in Fiction

Richard Strachan

Fantasy fiction, according to someone who should know, is many things: it is play, it is a pure game with no ulterior motive, it is something that delves into the Jungian archetypes which people our collective unconscious. It can be not mere escapism, but a wholly different approach to reality. Fantasy at its best is an interior journey, past the borders of a realm we uneasily patrol whenever we fall asleep. 'It is not anti-rational, but para-rational... its affinity is not with daydream, but with dream.'[1]

What if that dream is not your own though? What if that interior world of colour and archetypes and heightened, surre-alistic reality belongs to someone else, and you are only visiting? How do you journey inwards into someone else's dream?

* * *

---

1   Ursula K. Le Guin, 'From Elfland to Poughkeepsie' (1973).

If you had told me, as a struggling writer twenty years ago, that my first professionally published book would be a Warhammer tie-in novel called *Warcry Catacombs: Blood of the Everchosen*, I probably would have killed myself. I was obsessed with American novelists like Saul Bellow, Philip Roth, John Updike. I dug deep into the reformulations of post-war English fiction, from William Golding to J.G. Ballard, V.S. Naipaul to Martin Amis. I revered Iris Murdoch. I wanted to be Henry James, or James Joyce. I had no interest in fantasy at all, and I certainly didn't want to write in that most despised of forms: the *tie-in novel*, about as low down the literary hierarchy as you could get. Tie-in fiction was just the cheap novelisations of Hollywood blockbusters, or the preserve of sci-fi nerds who couldn't accept that their favourite TV programme had been cancelled and was never coming back. It wasn't literature. Fantasy wasn't literature. It was, as Le Guin (and before her Tolkien) cheerfully admitted, sheer escapism.

Now, though, I'm not so sure that writing tie-in Warhammer fiction didn't in fact save my life. Or, if that's to load it with more weight than it can bear, save my writing life at the very least. It was a far more varied landscape than I at first understood. There was greater freedom within it for staking your own claims and carving out your own territory. Although it operated on ground sowed by other hands, there was space enough to plough your own furrow. If I ever thought about it at all, I assumed that tie-in fiction was only a step up from copywriting. At its best, though, it could be something akin to the ever-evolving shared universe of mainstream American comics. For almost a century, superheroes like Batman, Superman, Wonder Woman, Captain America, Spider-Man, et cetera *ad nauseam*, have been shaped by dozens of different hands, each writer and artist bringing their own personal interpretation to those characters, and helping to reflect the changing social and cultural conditions under which they operated. To write for DC or Marvel, Dark Horse or IDW, is not to be despised. To write scripts for *Star Trek*, or *The Legend of Vox Machina*, would be a thrilling career opportunity. Is tie-in fiction, where the writer is being asked to fill in the blanks of a shared universe, really any different?

* * *

As the name suggests, tie-in fiction has always been connected to an originating 'IP', the intellectual property of a parent media organisation or creator. It had its modern start in the 1960s and 1970s, in the straightforward novelisations of films and television series, from Alan Dean Foster's 1976 recreation of a soon-to-be-released sci-fi movie called *Star Wars*, to the photo-novels and novelisations of original series *Star Trek* episodes. Foster's *Star Wars: From the Adventures of Luke Skywalker* (originally credited to George Lucas) was a massive bestseller, and arguably contributed to the enthusiasm with which the film was received when it arrived in cinemas in 1977. The *Star Trek* novelisations were written by luminaries including Harlan Ellison and Gene Roddenberry himself. In the UK, Terence Dicks was a prolific writer of *Doctor Who* novels, turning many of his own scripts into prose for Target Books, a publisher that specialised in film and TV novelisations for a teenage readership. This was an era before the availability of video, when television repeats were rare; if you missed an episode of your favourite TV programme, or if you didn't catch a film at the cinema, then it was likely you would never get a chance to see it again. The novelisation was a way for fans to experience an absence.

Tie-in fiction seems to operate best when its parent IP is in a state of uncertainty or abeyance, though. In television, when the originating form is cancelled or on hiatus, tie-in fiction becomes a sort of interstitial detailing between larger blocks of production. There was an extraordinary flowering of original *Doctor Who* fiction between the TV series cancellation in 1989 and its reboot in 2005, with Virgin Publishing and BBC Books following the continued adventures of Sylvester McCoy's Seventh Doctor, and then Paul McGann's Eighth Doctor following the abortive TV movie in 1996. Virgin's 'Past Doctor Adventures' drew on the whole range of the Doctor's previous iterations, and many of these novels and stories were written by people who would then go on to write for the 2005 series, including Russell T. Davies, Mark Gatiss, Chris Boucher and Gareth Roberts. These stories were arguably more inventive and interesting than the tamer, more family-friendly scripts produced for television.

Tie-in fiction doesn't need to be tied to a larger corporate IP, and can act as an expansion on the worlds and ideas of the original creator when they are no longer there to guide them. The prolific pulp writer Robert E. Howard's most famous creation, Conan the Cimmerian, has taken on a life of his own, well beyond the bounds of Howard's twenty-one original stories. Quite apart from Conan's expansion into film, television, video games, RPGs and board games, his written adventures were continued under the aegis of L. Sprague de Camp, Lin Carter and Harry Turtledove, among many, many others, with several new Conan novels being written in the 1980s by fantasy author Robert Jordan. (Tim Waggoner, James Lovegrove and Tim Lebbon have continued Conan's adventures into the present day, courtesy of Titan Books.) H.P. Lovecraft, Howard's *Weird Tales* stablemate, is another writer whose relatively paltry number of original stories has now been dwarfed by a vast quantity of cosmic 'Cthulhu Mythos' fiction; stories that draw on the aesthetics and tone, if not the exact detail, of his work. With his Conan novels, Robert Jordan was an important contributor to the idea of tie-in fiction as the exploration of a shared universe rather than the strict propping-up of an existing IP, and it's an interesting irony that his own Wheel of Time series would be concluded by another hand after his death (in this case the equally prolific fantasy author Brandon Sanderson).

These are all cases where the tie-in writer has the opportunity to flesh out details that were perhaps only sketched in by their originators. The reader understands exactly what they are going to get when they pick up a Conan comic or a collection of 'Lovecraftian' short stories: the expectation that they will see Conan, with gigantic melancholies and gigantic mirth, treading the jewelled thrones of the earth under his sandalled feet, or harried scholars psychologically crushed by the revelation that vast cosmic forces are pressing down on mute, unthinking humanity. Beyond that, the white spaces on the map are there to be filled in. Conan can press forward into the forgotten deserts and forests of the Hyborian Age, and Lovecraft's scholars can become hard-bitten pulp detectives or occult investigators, travelling well beyond the bounds of New England while still retaining their origins in those old books of forgotten lore.

* * *

Tie-in fiction, then, despite its long and occasionally ignoble history, was a form that didn't trouble my waking mind. Fantasy more generally was a place to which I had no intention of travelling. How did the two things become mixed, and offer me my first real entry into paid professional writing?

The motive was as mundane as any that makes a young and ambitious writer put pen to paper: I wanted to see my words in print. I wanted to know that other people were reading them, people perhaps not even related to me, although I soon found that this was harder than it seemed. Every now and then I would place a short story in a magazine or anthology, or even in the shortlist for a competition, but I would write novel after novel and fail to interest any agents or publishers in my work. For the most part these novels sat at the more innovative or speculative end of literary fiction; closer perhaps to what Zadie Smith called 'constructive deconstruction' rather than 'lyrical realism' in her groundbreaking 2008 essay 'Two Paths for the Novel'.[2] (To stake either claim would be to ludicrously over-estimate what I was writing in this period, though, which was more like sub-J.G. Ballard or an unholy blend of Martin Amis and William T. Vollmann.)

Many frustrating years passed while I pursued this model, the only one available for writers who want to be traditionally published. It felt as if my entire motive for writing fiction was only to see it bound between hard or soft covers. Eventually, I realised that I wasn't writing because I had anything particular to say or any personal aesthetic to explore, or even for the sheer joy of the pursuit, but because my sense of self was intimately bound up with the idea that someone might want to publish it.

I was now at the point of confluence where desperation and opportunity meet, perfectly primed to respond when I saw that Games Workshop's Black Library imprint was opening its submissions process for new writers. In 2018, I decided to apply.

Given everything I've said about the type of writer I wanted to be, it might seem strange that this open submissions process would even cross my path, let alone that I would roll up my sleeves and sketch out some proposals. By this point, though, and perhaps even as a reaction against the frustrating failures of my writing, I had re-embraced an old interest in Warhammer. My eldest daughter was about six years old at the time, and I had the idea that we could find some vaguely hobby-ish pursuit to undertake together after her baby sister was born. Board games, perhaps, or some kind of collectable card game, some-

---

2   www.nybooks.com/articles/2008/11/20/two-paths-for-the-novel/

thing that we could bond over. I had been a keen modeller and wargamer between the ages of ten and fifteen, in Games Workshop's Golden Age of the late 1980s and early 1990s. I had spent many an hour painting dwarfs and skeletons for my Warhammer Fantasy army, or Space Marines and Orks for my Warhammer 40,000 collection, or playing games like Blood Bowl, Space Hulk and Adeptus Titanicus; models and games that were assiduously packed away the very moment I got my first girlfriend, and which are now lost after one too many house moves. It seemed a natural step to pop into the Edinburgh branch of Games Workshop one Saturday and pick up a starter set for Warhammer Fantasy's newly rebranded iteration: 'Warhammer Age of Sigmar'. It was an easy transition to devote the hours I had spent on writing to hours spent on painting model soldiers, mastering the art after months of devoted practice, building armies of noble Stormcast Eternals, grizzled Fyreslayers, bloodthirsty Khorne barbarian berserkers, and (my favourite, and the only army not to eventually find its way onto eBay) the diseased, pustulant warriors of the Maggotkin of Nurgle. Never mind that my daughter soon lost all interest in the models or the game; I was absolutely hooked. I was soon travelling to tournaments to play likeminded enthusiasts, and doing what I thought by your late thirties was virtually impossible – making new friends. On my fortieth birthday I even travelled down to the Mecca of wargaming: Warhammer World in Nottingham, the world HQ of Games Workshop, where I took part in a two-day tournament and came a creditable 70th or so, out of over a hundred participants.

Writing for Black Library felt like a natural next step. I sent in my pitch for a short story set in the Age of Sigmar, along with the first 500 words, and then I waited for the response. It was only much later that I recognised this was perhaps the first indication that my need to write hadn't been completely suppressed. I had spotted an opportunity and decided to take it, combining a current with a very old and well-established obsession.

I progressed through the first round of submissions, being invited to expand my story by another 500 words and provide a more detailed outline, and with minimal friction I was soon asked to write a story for the new 'Warhammer Horror' line of fiction. This was to be character-based, a more ground-level view than the cosmic or planetary scale on which Warhammer's overarching narratives generally operated. I signed a contract, submitted a story, went through a couple of rounds of professional editing, and then next year I had the tremendous pleasure of receiving my author copies of the anthology, something which almost outweighed the pleasure I felt at actually getting paid for my work.

And soon they were asking for more. Further short stories followed, and a novella. My two main editors were obviously steeped in the traditions of the Warhammer IP, but their approach to my work was as professional as any editor in a more traditional publisher; they were concerned with narrative beats, character arcs, description, pacing, structure. They knew how to lean into my strengths and steer me away from my weaknesses in writing this kind of fiction. Soon I was being asked to write novels for them as well, and after three years of free-lance work, during which I was able to leave my job and do this full-time, I had seven hardback novels on my shelves, as well as multiple anthologies, to show for it. I wrote about duelling Chaos warbands in the hellish Eightpoints (the aforementioned *Warcry Catacombs: Blood of the Everchosen*); noble aelves strug-gling against corruption (*The End of Enlightenment*); the adven-tures of two hard-bitten, father-and-daughter witch hunters (*Hallowed Ground*); and many more. I had access to research material from the Games Workshop studio eighteen months in advance, poring over PDFs of rulebooks and campaign books well before anyone else got to see them. Sometimes novels and stories could be standalone tales with no particular connection to Games Workshop's current release schedule. At other times, they would explicitly tie in to a new edition of the main games or a campaign, and would be published alongside it. I was expected to highlight characters or locations that would feature in these new releases, but beyond that I had great freedom of action to take the stories in any direction I wished. The characters of Galen and Doralia Ven Denst, for example, the two witch hunters from *Hallowed Ground* and its sequel, *Temple of Silence*, first appeared in the *Broken Realms* series of studio-produced campaign books, but it was my novels that gave them a more detailed backstory: a history of PTSD and alcoholism on Doralia's part, and a strained personal relationship due to Galen's relentless training of his daughter after her mother's brutal death. There were certain guard rails within which these stories had to operate, but I was at liberty to write what I wanted.

* * *

Or was I? If the IP in question is still under corporate control, how much freedom of movement does the tie-in writer really have? The universe that was expanded by dozens of authors in the *Star Wars* novels and comics of the 1980s and 1990s was cruelly foreshortened and retconned out of existence by the time the *Star Wars* prequels and sequels were released. The *Doctor Who* novels eventually went out of print, and were replaced by a new run of more commercial and more explicitly relevant BBC-guided titles. In these cases, tie-in fiction went from being the long-term project of enthusiasts with a personal connection to the material, to a subsidiary concern explicitly designed to bolster the originating IP. Games Workshop is certainly no different. Marc Gascoigne, the first managing editor of GW's 'Black Library' when it was set up in the 1990s, noted that one of the main aims when preparing Warhammer fiction is that it not only fits the tone and detail of the Warhammer worlds, but that it also doesn't contradict the details of the 'current version' of the tabletop game.[3] The fantasy and sci-fi miniatures produced by Games Workshop are the real source of its income, and the pillar on which its success is built; everything else, in the final analysis, is just the scaffolding around that central corporate edifice.

When corporate constraints like this take precedence, does the writer's journey into this shared realm, these shared dreams, become more akin to a package holiday than an explorer's

---

3   warpstone.org/pdfs/interviews/marcgascoigne.pdf

expedition? Rather than setting forth with machete and pith helmet into the untamed wilds, the writer follows a tour guide along well-trodden paths, dutifully noting and photographing the expected sights. Does the very word 'constraint' here offer a problem or a challenge, especially when talking of a form like fantasy, which is, after all, supposed to be about the freest play of the imagination? In other words, is constraint a way of stifling invention, or, like the rules of a sonnet, does it provide the boundaries within which the imagination can take flight?

The problem, I think, is that we associate imaginative freedom with a sense of the untrammelled, with an absence of borders and limits, but in a sense all writers are constrained by the boundaries of their form. Crucially, and in a way that perhaps few writers would want to admit, these boundaries are more often industrial or commercial than not. Production imperatives influence the direction of tie-in fiction as much as mainstream or literary fiction, it's just that nobody involved pretends otherwise. A short story written for a competition can only be so long; a novel will be contracted by a publisher for 90,000 words, because the profit-and-loss spreadsheet sets out the acceptable production costs against the likely return for anything longer. Even dreams are bounded by periods of waking.

For my own part, there is an element of truth to this, but it's not the whole truth. There were times when I could do as I pleased, and times when I had to adhere more closely to established lore, but they were almost always connected to the release schedule of the wider company. Black Library existed to reflect the worlds of Games Workshop's miniatures, and it was in navigating a course through that crowded schedule that you could sometimes find uninhabited isles of narrative freedom. Of all the novels I wrote for Black Library, I'm most proud of *The Vulture Lord*, a story about the tragic undead king Zothar Athrabis and his tyrannical rule over an isolated city as he attempts to recapture the soul of his dead son. Zothar's form was drawn from Age of Sigmar's range of undead Ossiarch Bonereaper miniatures, but the character was my own, and the culture, history and religion of the city was entirely my own invention. Drawing on Greek myth, Zoroastrianism, ideas of sacrifice and rebellion, I think to this day that *The Vulture Lord* is a pretty good standalone fantasy novel, one which could be enjoyed by readers who know nothing of Warhammer beyond the name.

At the other extreme, my penultimate novel was an instalment in the continuing adventures of Black Library's most enduring character, Gotrek Gurnisson. A taciturn dwarf trollslayer with a death wish, Gotrek was previously an inhabitant of the old Warhammer Fantasy world, a quasi-medieval landscape loosely based on fifteenth-century Europe. He had been ported over to Age of Sigmar and its more cosmic, planar setting to provide a ground-level perspective on its sometimes bewildering high fantasy universe, and was by far the most popular character in Black Library's stable. In fact, his 1999 debut *Trollslayer* (by William King) was the very first novel published under the Black Library label. As such, writing my novel *Blightslayer* was the first time I had sensed a sterner editorial eye peering over my shoulder. Gotrek absolutely had to act in a certain way. The Mortal Realms of the Age of Sigmar absolutely had to reflect the way he would see them. The company was exerting a stronger influence on the work than I had previously felt, and the experience was from start to finish a frustrating one.

There is another force that exerts a stronger influence on the writing of tie-in fiction, though, one more closely tied to the production imperatives mentioned above than to either a corporation's interest in protecting its IP or the desires of a writer to stamp their authority on what can seem like mere work for hire. That force is rooted in the wellspring of tie-in fiction: the shared universes of the pulp magazines, where writers like Robert E. Howard and H.P. Lovecraft found their audience in the 1920s. Tie-in fiction is essentially pulp fiction for the late twentieth and early twenty-first century, and like pulp fiction it has a voracious appetite. As a production model it is high-volume and fast-paced, and it rewards people who can not only write with facility, but who can also write very, very quickly.

When I was first asked to write a novel for Black Library, I was given ten weeks to hand in a draft. Given that each of my previous, failed novels had taken me around three years, I thought this schedule was essentially impossible. As it turns out, being paid for your work is an intense motivator. Like an actor breezily confirming his horse-riding experience before taking a part, I waved all difficulties away and got to work.

It's essentially a question of mathematics. Producing 90,000 words in ten weeks, assuming you write every day, is roughly 1,285 words a day. If you give yourself the weekends off, it's

1,800 words a day. Broken down like this it doesn't sound too bad, but then literature isn't a numbers game. What about inspiration, the crafting of sentences, cadence, the exploratory sense of an unfolding narrative? What about characters who seem to come alive and go in their own unforeseen directions?

Pulp fiction doesn't care about any of that. What counts is pace. Pace is everything. Pace determines whether your story works or fails, and you only get that sense of pace through writing as fast as you possibly can.

Writing fast, to cover a minimum 2,000 words a day, means writing smart. I soon learned that much of the work has to be front-loaded. A novel pitch can be expanded into a synopsis, which can be expanded into an outline. It helps if you've thought through your main and minor characters a little before starting, that you've absorbed something about the environment where the story is taking place, and that you've got a basic, intuitive grasp of narrative structure. A week of work setting all this up will save you months in the long run.

Writing fast can seem like a mere logistics problem, of harnessing a Stakhanovite work ethic where quality becomes measured by quantity, but as I worked on these novels, I also found that this sense of pace can have a strangely beneficial effect on the style. High fantasy pulp fiction is, on the whole, not going to be particularly subtle. There's no space here for the Hemingway iceberg theory, or the intellectually rambunctious, allusive style of a Saul Bellow. It is overblown in the best possible way, and when you are typing almost faster than you can think, you gain access to a style of real melodramatic force: a weirdly poetic technique of both sonority and precision, which would seem ludicrous in any other context. It's telling that *The Vulture Lord*, the Warhammer novel I'm most proud of, and one that I tried to write in a more measured indirect style, is the one that has received by far the worst reviews and sales of any of them. *Blood of the Everchosen*, which makes Robert E. Howard sound like E.M. Forster, was far more of a hit.

Writing those novels under those high-volume conditions was like the best, most compressed creative writing degree I could possibly have taken. I learned more about writing narrative and character in those three years than I had done in all my writing life prior to entering that open submissions call, and they were lessons that I took forward when I knew my time working for Black Library was over. I had gone as far with it as I wanted to go, and I ploughed everything I had learned back into my own work. The desire to write had been reignited by actually writing for a living, and I was soon working on the book that was to become my 'real' debut.[4] A historical gothic novel, it was crucially a step back from 'constructive deconstruction' and the pseudo-experimental novels that I had failed to publish before. It was lyrical realism, certainly, but it drew on elements of the fantastical as well, the ghost story, the hint of other worlds that are forever out of reach. It revelled in character and plot in a way I would never have attempted before I plunged into the ferment of pulp fiction. It may have taken me slightly longer than ten weeks to write, but its bones are clothed in the sinews of Warhammer all the same, just a little bit.

---

4   *The Unrecovered* (Raven Books, 2025)

* * *

As for fantasy fiction more generally, I came to appreciate the greater role it had played in my writing and reading than I had previously understood. After all, when choosing a hobby to explore with my daughter (and then to take forward by myself), I had leaned towards Warhammer's fantasy range rather than its sci-fi offering. Landscape and memory, changing seasons, characters surviving through their own physical and emotional efforts, a sense of magic – these were all things I associated with the fantasy genre, and they had long roots in my creative life. My mother had been a great fan of fantasy fiction, and when I was growing up her shelves were a source of books with thrilling and sometimes ludicrous titles: *Curse of the Mistwraith*, *The Birthgrave*, *Dragonflight*. *The Lord of the Rings* was perhaps the one book I had read and reread more than any other. I loved Mervyn Peake and Ray Bradbury, Clive Barker and Le Guin's Earthsea novels. Like half the world, I had watched *Game of Thrones*. Fantasy, I understood, had always been there in the background; a memory waiting to be tapped, a realm waiting for me to re-explore. I had been creatively asleep for a long time. Fantasy, it turned out, was what I needed to wake up.

The Door in the Mound

Katherine Langrish

I began writing fantasy when I was nine years old, having fallen deeply in love with the seven Chronicles of Narnia. Next to finding my own way into that wonderful world, the thing I wanted most would have been an eighth Narnia book to read, but since C.S. Lewis had died I decided to write one for myself, and after that I never stopped. I am still writing for the child I was then and for older iterations of her; I'm also writing for the adult I am now. So what is children's fantasy, and what do children want from it? Friendship, loyalty, magic and danger are the basics, occurring in a created world which feels *real*, for as Joan Aiken says in her book *The Way to Write for Children*:

> It is the writer's duty to demonstrate to children that the world is *not* a simple place. Far from it. The world is an infinitely rich, strange, confusing, wonderful, cruel, mysterious, beautiful, inexplicable riddle. We too are a riddle. We don't know where we come from or where we are going.[1]

---

1   Aiken, Joan, *The Way to Write for Children* (St Martin's Press, 1982) p.16.

All fiction is to some extent fantasy. No matter whether it's set in contemporary London, Middle-earth, or another planet, writers of fiction make things up. Every novel is itself a portal into other worlds and other lives. The main difference between fantasy and realism is that those of us who write fantasy have more to play with. To use John Donne's words, we are 'born to strange sights, things impossible to see',[2] such as falling stars, mermaids, talking animals, dragons, unicorns. How lucky are we? We hold a magic mirror up to this world we live in, and those who stare deeply enough into it will see themselves. Fantasy views reality through a different lens, and can be the more powerful for it.

As a genre, fantasy covers a vast range, and children's fantasy is no different. Some are set in self-contained worlds like Ursula K. Le Guin's Earthsea, or Garth Nix's Old Kingdom; others are like the Narnia series, in which children from this world pass through portals into magical lands. There are animal fantasies as different from one another as *The Wind in the Willows* and *Watership Down*, and fantasies in which contemporary life is penetrated by ancient magic such as the Welsh legends of Susan Cooper's *The Dark is Rising*, and Catherine Fisher's *The Clockwork Crow* and its sequels. Some are based on fairy tales, some are set in the reinvented past, present and speculative futures of our own world, and some are impossible to categorise, like Tove Jansson's gentle, strangely melancholy Moomintroll titles. And there are fantasies drawn from legends and cultures other than

2   Donne, John, 'Song': www.poetryfoundation.org/poems/44127/song-go-and-catch-a-falling-star

white Euro-American, by authors like S.F. Said, Sarwat Chadda, Shveta Thakrar, Tomi Adeyemi, B.B. Alston, Tracy Deonn and many others, in whose pages children previously unrepresented in fantasy can see themselves. It is a rich field.

One distinct difference between writing for adults and writing for children is the simple fact that children grow up. Successful writers for adults may gain followers who will stay with them for many years, but the readership for children's writers is in constant turnover. Eight-year-olds become twelve-year-olds who become teenagers who become... Say you're writing a trilogy for middle grade: by the time the third book is published, many of the children who enjoyed the first will already have moved on, so you must continually appeal to new generations. Then again, children vary greatly in reading ability and tastes. Though you need at least a rough idea what age-group you're writing for, middle grade and YA are simply approximate labels. As C.S. Lewis remarked in 1952:

[T]he neat sorting-out of books into age-groups, so dear to publishers, has only a very sketchy relation with the habits of any real readers. Those of us who are blamed when old for reading childish books were blamed when children for reading books too old for us.[3]

And nothing much has changed. There are eight-year-olds who will happily devour Philip Pullman's challenging fantasy

---

3   Lewis, C.S., 'On Three Ways of Writing for Children' in *On Stories and Other Essays on Literature*, ed. Walter Hooper (Harcourt, 1982) p.36.

His Dark Materials, others of the same age prefer the slapstick fun of Dav Pilkey's *Captain Underpants*, and some will love both. But though a confident eight-year-old may tackle *Northern Lights*, her teenage brother or sister is unlikely to return to *Captain Underpants*: the richness, darkness and nuance of Pullman's writing offers so much more to older readers.

YA fantasy is generally edgier and scarier than that of middle grade, and can be sadder too. Teenagers enjoy tragedy and heartbreak as long as there's also romance: star-crossed lovers will always be box-office. At the end of Pullman's *The Amber Spyglass*, the protagonists Lyra and Will are parted, although deeply in love. They belong to different worlds, and the portals between must be closed to halt the flow of Dust. They can never be together again, but one thing both softens and accentuates the tragedy – they promise that every year in their own version of Oxford, each will visit a particular bench in the Botanic Gardens. 'If we could come here,' says Lyra:

> '—if we could come here at the same time, just for an hour or something, then we could pretend we were close again – because we *would* be close, if you sat *here* and I sat just *here* in my world—'
>
> 'Yes,' he said, 'as long as I live, I'll come back. Wherever I am in the world, I'll come back here—'
>
> 'On Midsummer Day,' she said. 'At midday. As long as I live. As long as I live…'[4]

---

4   Pullman, Philip, *The Amber Spyglass* (Alfred A Knopf, 2000) p.507, 508.

It is genuinely moving; the separation feels as painful as Lyra's separation from her daemon Pantalaimon. And readers love it. Some years ago, a young Australian girl wrote to thank me for my Troll trilogy, a fantasy set in a Viking-Scandinavia-that-never-was, peopled with creatures from Nordic folklore like trolls, nixies and nisses.[5] She explained that she'd been in the lowest reading group at school and had never got through an entire book before, but she'd loved the Troll titles so much she'd finished all of them and was now a really good reader. Well, those three books average sixty to seventy thousand words each and the vocabulary is fairly advanced, so I reckon she could always have been a good reader: perhaps the trouble was that she hadn't been helped to find books she would really enjoy. That is important, for the books we love as children often remain with us for life. They become part of us.

For example, Alan Garner writes brilliantly for both children and adults, and much of his work is based on folklore and legends. His most recent adult title, *Treacle Walker*,[6] is a wonderful, complex, deceptive, riddling tale which incorporates the character 'Stonehenge Kit the Ancient Brit', a figure whose adventures in the weekly comic *Knockout* he read in March 1941 as a six-year-old 'lying in bed in an isolation hospital, recovering from measles, whooping cough and meningitis'. He could read the speech balloons, but suddenly found he could decode the lengthier captions beneath the pictures: 'I fell back

5   Langrish, Katherine, *Troll Fell* (HarperCollins, 2004); *Troll Mill* (HarperCollins, 2005); *Troll Blood* (HarperCollins, 2007).

6   Garner, Alan, *Treacle Walker* (Fourth Estate, 2021).

in the bed and stared through the window at a silver barrage balloon hanging in the sky above Manchester and couldn't stop trembling.'[7] That is how important children's reading can be, regardless of whether or not some adults see it.

Many children enjoy funny stories, but for those who want something more, a good deal of darkness and jeopardy can be packed into middle grade stories, and even quite young children may enjoy age-appropriate shivers. At the age of five or six I would read the tales of Beatrix Potter aloud to my teddy-bears and dolls. My favourite was *The Tale of Mr Tod*, in which the disreputable badger Tommy Brock kidnaps seven baby rabbits, breaks into the empty 'house' of Mr Tod the fox (equally disreputable), shuts the babies up overnight in a cold oven, and goes to sleep with his boots on in Mr Tod's bed. Arriving at dusk to rescue the babies, Peter Rabbit and Benjamin Bunny find the bedroom window has been recently opened – 'there were fresh dirty footmarks upon the window-sill'. This passage follows:

The sun had set; an owl began to hoot in the wood. There were many unpleasant things lying about, that had much better have been buried; rabbit bones and skulls, and chickens' legs and other horrors. It was a shocking place, and very dark.[8]

---

7   Garner, Alan, *The Guardian*, Friday, 3 December 2021: www.theguard-ian.com/books/2021/dec/03/alan-garner-the-chronicles-of-narnia-are-atro-ciously-written

8   Potter, Beatrix, *The Tale of Mr Tod* (Frederick Warne & Co. Ltd, 1912) p.39.

I really doubt a modern editor would permit such a gruesome vision in a book for little children, but back then I found it thrilling, not frightening, and it gets even darker when, after rigging a metal pail of water to drop on the sleeping Tommy Brock, Mr Tod thinks he has killed him:

'I will bury that nasty person in the hole which he has dug. I will bring my bedding out and dry it in the sun,' said Mr Tod... 'I will get soft soap, and monkey soap, and all sorts of soap, and soda and scrubbing brushes...; and carbolic to remove the smell.'[9]

In the last few pages Tommy Brock and Mr Tod tumble fighting down the hillside, giving the two rabbits the chance to rush in and save the babies. Stories for small children must end happily with danger averted, so all is well... but there has to *be* some danger first.

In this respect, writing for children has much in common with fairy tales, which along with Beatrix Potter's are often some of the first stories children encounter. Fairy tales offer a version of the world as we might like it to be, in which the innocent and good always (eventually) triumph, while the wicked are punished. Children expect this. After taking two children to see Maeterlinck's fairy-tale play, *The Blue Bird*, G.K. Chesterton famously wrote that the children felt:

---

9   Ibid p.77, 78.

dissatisfied with it because it did not end with a Day of Judgement; because it was never revealed to the hero and heroine that the dog had been faithful and the cat faithless. For children are innocent and love justice; while most of us are wicked and naturally prefer mercy.[10]

'It isn't fair!' is the perennial cry of an injured child, and fairy tales insist upon justice – not mercy. They are grittier than many people realise, and do not ignore the dark side of life. Fairy-tale families are not safe. They are dysfunctional, full of generational tension, threatened by bad fairies, haunted by inconvenient prophecies. Parents abandon their children in the woods, make them perform impossible tasks, saddle them with obligations incurred before their birth, as happens to Rapunzel. Mothers die, replaced by wicked stepmothers like Snow White's – balanced on the male side by a whole parade of unreasonable, greedy, weak or incestuous fathers, and I do mean fathers not stepfathers. The best course of action for a young person in a fairy tale is to leave home as soon as possible.

Unwatered down, fairy tales are uncompromising, and children still lucky enough to read or hear the unbowdlerised versions waste little sympathy on the baddies, even when these wicked people dance to death in red-hot shoes or are rolled down hills in nail-studded barrels. A child's sympathy is with the hero or heroine – the underdog who comes out on top. Orphans are a recurrent theme in children's literature because (in fiction at least)

---

10   Chesterton, G.K., 'On Household Gods and Goblins' in *The Coloured Lands* (Sheed & Ward, 1938) p.195.

dead, absent or neglectful parents make space for child protagonists to shine. Orphanhood grants them agency, and establishes a
bond of sympathy between reader and character. Another reason
why children are generally satisfied with fairy-tale retribution is
that they know fairy tales *are not real*. They don't pretend to be.
They are set far away and long ago, and lack spatial and temporal
reference points. Characters are 'the lad', 'the maiden', 'the
princess', 'the child'; any proper names are descriptive (Snow-
White, Rose-Red) or else very common (Gretel, Hans, Kate,
Jack). Worldbuilding is minimal: a castle is a castle, a forest is
dark, a princess is as *beautiful as the day* – and that's it. Fairy tales
operate in what compared with the novel is a two-dimensional
world. So – 'Could it really happen?' – 'No!'

Novels by contrast create detailed three-dimensional worlds
and crave the reader's belief, which is usually given. It is not
difficult to find, online, grown-up fans of the Harry Potter
books reliving the bitter childhood disappointment when their
invitations to Hogwarts never arrived.[11] At nine or ten years old,
with most of my friends I was almost certain Narnia did really
exist – somewhere. Because it had to! But another part of me
knew it was impossible, and so *Tales of Narnia* came into existence in the shape of an old notebook filled with stories, poems
and pictures. It was my attempt to get there by a different way,
but it didn't quite work. (Just incidentally, children often do

---

11   www.reddit.com/r/harrypotter/comments/7q514m/was_anyone_else_
disappointed_when_they_hadnt/?rdt=47634
www.quora.com/How-many-people-wished-and-hoped-a-letter-from-
Hogwarts-would-come-to-them-on-their-10th-birthday

write stories in imitation of books they love. Around the same age, our daughters, fans of Jacqueline Wilson's gritty and funny middle grade novels, were writing first-person narratives for their primary school about drunken mums and absent dads. We hoped their teachers recognised the source.)

I ransacked Narnia for plots and characters, borrowed entire sentences, made careful copies of Pauline Baynes's maps for the endpapers, and in the process made two useful discoveries. First, that I couldn't write as well as Lewis. Second, that *writing* a story is a different experience from reading one. Reading, I was immersed in the world of Lewis's imagination, the enchantment was entire. But whilst writing I was aware of being on the outside of my story, creating and constructing it. It felt rather like being Alice in the White Rabbit's house, with one arm out of the window and a foot up the chimney – too big to fit. I loved writing my stories, but it wasn't the same thing as diving headfirst into somebody else's marvellous world, an experience which is one of the great delights of fantasy.

It is our job, as writers of fantasy, to open doors from the everyday into the magical. So how do we make our fantasy worlds so real that the reader just *has* to believe in them? By thinking them through and through, by putting in lots of work. It's not only about drawing maps, useful as they are. What *kind* of a world are you creating? Who is in charge, how is it run, what threatens it, what threatens your characters? Infused with the spirit of William Blake, S.F. Said's magnificent *Tyger*[12] is set

---

12   Said, S.F., *Tyger* (David Fickling Books, 2022)

in an imperialist, racist London where a brown-skinned boy and girl help a mystic, wounded Tyger escape from those hunting her. It's a world of dark satanic mills and prejudice, but a story of courage, loyalty and friendship. Early in the book a terrifying cut-throat chases young Adam Alhambra into a ruined warehouse. Then: 'Something erupted out of the darkness, moving so fast, he saw only a blur at first.' It's the Tyger, whose roar sends the cut-throat running. Adam stares at her, 'his senses fill[ing] with a sweet, high, musky scent, like honeysuckle growing wild. In her presence, everything else just melted away, even his fear.' Then he sees blood running from an arrow sticking out of her shoulder. Carefully he snaps off the shaft and draws the arrowhead 'inch by inch from her flesh and fur':

The animal sighed a huge sigh of relief. She slumped to the ground and began to lick her shoulder, licking and licking with her tongue, trying to stop the bleeding as the rain streamed down outside.

Adam slumped down beside her. His knees felt weak as water. But somehow, he had done it. He had got the arrow out.

'I think you're going to be all right,' he said, to himself as much as her.

And that was when she spoke, in a voice as clear and close as his own heart, thumping in his throat.

'I thank you,' she said. 'I thank you, oh Guardian, for your help.'[13]

---

13   Ibid., p.15.

These few pages feel all action, while simultaneously painting a London of dark alleys, ruined buildings, pouring rain and human cruelty. 'Slumped' is exactly the right verb for the relieved exhaustion of both Tyger and boy. That description of the arrow pulled 'inch by inch from her flesh and fur' is wincingly physical, and the phrase 'a voice as clear and close as his own heart' – *that* suggests much about the Tyger. (Also, the book is illustrated! Pictures are a welcome come-back to middle grade publishing and Dave McKean's strong, black-ink illustrations brilliantly complement the text.)

A reason the world of Narnia seemed to me so convincing is that much of its landscape is an idealised version of rural England or Ireland, both of which Lewis knew well. There's a wonderful moment when Lucy and Susan ride on Aslan's back:

> right across Narnia, in spring, down solemn avenues of beech and across sunny glades of oak, through wild orchards of snow-white cherry trees, past roaring waterfalls and mossy rocks and echoing caverns, up windy slopes alight with gorse bushes, and across the shoulders of heathery mountains and along giddy ridges, and down, down, down again into wild valleys and out into acres of blue flowers.[14]

The passage succeeds so well because it's not static, doesn't stop – sweeps us along in Aslan's joyous rush across the coun-

---

14   Lewis, C.S., *The Lion, the Witch and the Wardrobe* (Puffin Books, 1973) p.150.

tryside, up slopes, over mountains, 'down, down, down' to the Witch's castle – we hurtle along with them. A well-known rule of writing is to avoid using too many adjectives, but look at them piling up there – *solemn, sunny, wild, snow white, roaring, mossy, echoing, windy, heathery, giddy, blue* – all in one breathless sentence, and it works! Most of the words are stressed on the first syllable and can be spoken quickly so they sound light and speedy: if you're going to break the rules, break them big, but know what you're doing. Just as vivid are descriptions of other parts of the Narnian world, such as the hot desert sand that burns Shasta's bare foot in *The Horse and His Boy*, reminding us he's too poor to have shoes – the bleak snowy moors of *The Silver Chair*, and the brilliant Eastern Sea of *The Voyage of the Dawn Treader*.

J.R.R. Tolkien's Middle-earth is amazingly physical. I was thirteen when I first read *The Lord of the Rings*, and I hadn't much liked *The Hobbit* a few years earlier: I'd felt talked down to. The narrator was sometimes facetious, the elves sang silly songs, Gollum was too slimy and I wasn't keen on Bilbo. *The Lord of the Rings* blew all that away. This time there was no question that Tolkien was completely serious: the humour was never facetious and this utterly grounded world was a revelation. In Chapter 6 of *The Fellowship of the Ring*, the four hobbits try a shortcut through the Old Forest, which goes wrong from the start:

[T]he trees began to close in again, just where they had appeared from a distance to be thinner and less tangled. Then deep folds in the ground were discovered unexpectedly, like the ruts of great giant-wheels or wide moats and sunken roads long disused and choked with brambles. These lay usually right across their line of march, and could only be crossed by scrambling down and out again, which was troublesome and difficult with the ponies. Each time they climbed down they found the hollow filled with thick bushes and matted undergrowth, which somehow would not yield to the left... and they were forced to the right and downwards.[15]

There are far fewer adjectives here than in Lewis's gallop across Narnia but they are equally well chosen: *deep folds, wide moats, sunken road, thick bushes, matted undergrowth.* They feel slow and weighty, like obstacles. You linger over them. Good writing does more than one thing at a time, and again this is more than simple description. Those *ruts, moats, sunken roads long disused* transmit a shiver of unease, of danger. *Whose* roads? We never find out, but know in our bones that the Old Forest is inimical, unfriendly. I've had the thought for years that Middle-earth is so real you could dig a hole in the ground.

C.S. Lewis was succeeded in my teens by other authors I admired, whose style (but not characters) I tried to emulate. Alan Garner was one, and hopeless though it might seem, my efforts were not useless. Garner's landscapes really exist, his writing is rooted in the particular part of Cheshire where he and generations of his family have always lived and worked. I tried

---

15   Tolkien, J.R.R., *The Fellowship of the Ring* (George Allen and Unwin, 1969) p.125.

placing my own stories in landscapes I knew, though usually I'd disguise the names. Rather as art students were expected – are they still? – to sit in galleries copying Old Masters, almost unconsciously I was picking up some of the techniques of writing, learning the craft. (When later I began oral storytelling in schools, mostly fairy tales, I learned much about the stories the children really loved. They relished the gruesome bits.)

Nowadays creative writing courses and 'how to' books can teach many of these things, but nothing will replace reading contemporary children's fantasy, and plenty of it. It isn't safe to rely on memories of what you yourself read as a child. Those titles may have sparked your desire to write, but no matter how good they are, you need to know how modern children behave, think and speak. The Narnia stories are classics and much may be learned from them, but the four Pevensies belong to the 1950s. They are white upper-middle-class children who go to boarding schools, and their slang and assumptions are long out of date. Today's kids don't call one another by their last names as Jill Pole and Eustace Scrubb do in *The Silver Chair*, or say things like, 'Don't be a perfect beast,' or 'We've muffed the first Signs.'[16] Children in modern fiction are as likely to live in high-rise city blocks with parents who both go out to work as in some country village. In middle grade novels, girls and boys form alliances and make friends; in YA, romance often blooms: girls are strong and capable, boys are allowed to be vulnerable… Anyway, if you want to write modern children's fantasy, why wouldn't you want to read it too?

---

16   Lewis, C.S., *The Silver Chair* (Collins & Sons, 1990) p.40, 41.

Children's books get little review coverage and are not infrequently dismissed as nonsense unworthy of adult attention – even though thousands of adults regularly read children's literature, and children who love books are likely to become the very readers adult writers and publishers need. Whenever a book for children is so brilliant it *cannot* be ignored, the author is treated like some kind of phoenix, so rare they barely count as a children's writer at all. When Alan Garner's memoir *Where Shall We Run To?* was published in 2018, a *Guardian* reviewer exclaimed, 'He has never been just a children's writer; he's far richer, odder and deeper than that.' The same quote reappeared on the back of his 2021 novella *Treacle Walker*.[17] While it's true that neither title is aimed at children, that's no excuse for insulting an entire genre. As bestselling children's fantasy writer Katherine Rundell has wryly remarked: 'So that's what children's fiction is not: not rich or odd or deep…'[18]

'Not *just* a children's writer'? How ignorant that reviewer was. Frances Hardinge's many YA novels are beautifully written, vivid, dark and fascinating: her extraordinary fantasy *Deeplight*[19] won the Costa Book Award in 2019. It tells of a boy named Hark and his best friend Jelt, who scavenge a living on an island in the Myriad Archipelago, diving for relics of the sea-gods whose long-ago war devastated the islands. But something is rising from the Undersea, and when

17   Garner, Alan, *Treacle Walker* (Fourth Estate, 2021)

18   Rundell, Katherine, *Why You Should Read Children's Books, Even Though You Are So Old And Wise* (Bloomsbury, 2019) p.3.

19   Hardinge, Frances, *Deeplight* (Macmillan, 2019)

Jelt changes into something inhuman, Hark must act to save his friend… Philip Pullman's books, of course, need no introduction, and I've mentioned S.F. Said's wonderful *Tyger*,[20] and Catherine Fisher's *The Clockwork Crow*[21] which won the Tir nan-Og Award in 2018. Tracy Deonn's thrilling *Legendborn*[22] mingles 'Southern Black girl magic'[23] with Arthurian legend: following her mother's death, Black teenager Bree enrols at the University of South Carolina, where she witnesses a demon attack and discovers a secret magical society which exists to hunt demons down. The members are descendants of Arthur's knights – but can the 'Legendborn' be trusted? In B.B. Alston's *Amari and the Night Brothers*, Amari joins the magical Bureau of Supernatural Affairs hoping to find her missing brother. Reminiscent of the Harry Potter novels, and excellent fun, this story too explores difference, racism and prejudice. Polly Ho-Yen's *The Last Dragon*[24] is a delightful middle grade fantasy set in contemporary England (Milton Keynes, in fact). The last ever dragon leaves her egg with the heroine Yara, who believes it may cure her sick little sister. But the sinister Dragon Detection Squad is after it, and Yara and her non-binary friend Bertie must keep it safe at all costs. There are many more authors to discover.

20   Said, S.F., *Tyger* (David Fickling Books, 2022)

21   Fisher, Catherine, *The Clockwork Crow* (Firefly Press, 2018)

22   Deonn, Tracy, *Legendborn* (Simon & Schuster, 2020)

23   www.syfy.com/syfy-wire/get-recd-with-tracy-deonn-five-fantasy-reimag-inings-for-fangrrls-readers

24   Ho-Yen, Polly, *The Last Dragon* (Knights Of, 2024)

Children's fiction and fantasy often tackle what is scary, unfair or hard to understand, and this is right because children are complex beings. They have little power but strong feelings, and grapple with an adult world that can seem difficult and strange. Returning to the world of fairy tales for a moment, it's a realm in which the poor, powerless and down-trodden almost always win, but only after passing through many trials – climbing glass mountains, weaving shirts from nettles, stealing hairs from the Devil's head. This is the template for the plot and characters of many a fantasy, including the Harry Potter books and Frodo. 'Even the smallest person can make a difference,' as Galadriel says in the film of *The Lord of the Rings*. Is this unrealistic?

In *Don't Tell the Grown-ups: Subversive Children's Literature*, Alison Lurie describes the dull books considered suitable for her as a child of five in the early 1930s. One was *The Here and Now Story Book* by Lucy Sprague Mitchell: 'Inside I could read about the Grocery Man ("This is John's Mother. Good morning, Mr Grocery Man") and How Spot Found a Home. The children and parents in these stories were exactly like the ones I knew, only more boring.' She adds:

> After we grew up of course, we realised how unrealistic these stories had been. The simple, pleasant adult society they had prepared us for did not exist. As we suspected, the fairy tales had been right all along – the world was full of hostile, stupid giants and perilous castles and people who abandoned their children in the nearest forest. To

succeed in this world you needed some special skill or patronage, plus remarkable luck, and it didn't hurt to be very good-looking. The other qualities that counted were wit, boldness, stubborn persistence, and an eye for the main chance. Kindness to those in trouble was also advisable – you never knew who might be useful to you later on.[25]

Like Frodo's kindness to Gollum, perhaps?

There's a passage in Alan Garner's children's fantasy *Elidor* which for me sums up the 'how to?' of writing a convincing fantasy, regardless of whether for children or adults. The novel is based on the fairy-tale ballad *Childe Rowland*, published in 1814 by Robert Jamieson, who remembered it imperfectly from his childhood around 1770, though it's older than that. It's referenced in *King Lear* when Edgar pretends to be mad:

Childe Rowland to the Dark Tower came,
His word was still: 'Fie, foh and fum,
I smell the blood of a British man.'[26]

The last two lines refer to the dread cry of the King of Elfland, and the tale tells how young Childe Rowland kicks a football over a church, how his sister Helen runs widdershins around the church to retrieve it and vanishes into elfland, how

25   Lurie, Alison, *Don't Tell The Grown-ups: Subversive Children's Literature* (Bloomsbury, 1990) p.17, 18.

26   Shakespeare, William, *King Lear,* Act 3 Scene 4.

his two elder brothers set out to rescue her with advice from Merlin, which they forget to follow and so fail to return. Then Rowland sets out. He remembers Merlin's advice and is able to revive his dead brothers and bring his sister home.

In Garner's *Elidor*, four bored children, Nicholas, David, Helen and Roland, wander around 1960s Manchester to be out of the way while their parents move house. (Unlikely nowadays: another example of how things change.) They enter a demolition area of bomb damage and slums, where 'black in the wasteland stood a church. It was a plain Victorian building with buttresses and lancet windows, a steep roof, but no spire. And beside it were a mechanical excavator and a lorry.' Swiftly sketched, the important words are 'black in the wasteland': this is a perilous, liminal space. The children start playing with a football fished from underneath the lorry, someone starts a high thin tune on a fiddle across the street, and Roland kicks the ball right through the church window. Helen goes after it and doesn't return. Next David goes, then Nick. The music comes again and fades. Alone, Roland finds a broken side door and climbs into the church which smells 'of soot and cat'. There's no sign of his sister or brothers, and though glass from the broken window lies beneath it, no sign of the ball. 'The floorboards and joists had been taken away, everything movable had been ripped out down to the brick. The church was a cavern.'[27]

In an atmosphere of gathering menace, and *because* the wrecked church is so vividly drawn, we're ready to believe what

---

27   Garner, Alan, *Elidor* (Collins, 1965) p.20, 21.

happens next as Roland meets the fiddler and is drawn into the fairy world of Elidor – where in a nightmare moment he finds the empty fingers of his sister's woollen glove sticking out of the unbroken turf of the Mound of Vanwy. To rescue her and his brothers he must enter the doorless Mound, and the fiddler Malebron tells him he can make a door by visualising it, forcing it to *be*. 'Think of the door you know best,' he advises, and Roland thinks of the front door of his family's new house. With closed eyes he sees its paint-blisters, and the brass letter-flap he'd been cleaning on the previous day: he sees the word 'Letters' outlined in dried metal polish. And he imagines how strange it would look in the side of a hill. Then Malebron asks him if it's really there? Is it physical? Could he touch it?

'I think so,' said Roland.

'Then open your eyes. It is still there.'

'No. It's just a hill.'

'It is still there!'cried Malebron. 'It is real! You have made it with your mind! Your mind is real! You can see the door!'

Roland shut his eyes again. The door had a brick porch, and there was a house leek growing on the stone roof. His eyes were so tightly closed that he began to see coloured lights floating behind his lids and they were all shaped like the porch entrance... and behind them all, unmoving, the true porch, square-cut, solid.

'Yes,' said Roland. 'It's there. The door. It's real.'[28]

---

28   Garner, Alan, *Elidor* (Collins, 1965) p.39, 40.

In setting the front door of his new house in the side of the Mound, Roland inadvertently connects the two worlds of 1960s Manchester and the land of Elidor. His everyday front door becomes a portal into the sinister fairy world, and Elidor's power begins leaching through.

The blisters in the paint, the dried metal-polish around the letterbox, the *detail...* this passage is not only brilliantly written, it is the blueprint of how to create fantasy. Roland's effort to place that door in the side of the Mound – to make it real, tactile, functional – is precisely the effort a writer must bring to her or his work. It is our job first to imagine and then communicate our fantasy worlds so clearly that the reader sees, hears, tastes, experiences what is happening. The old wardrobe, the smell of mothballs, the fur coats, the unexpected depth – *where's the back?* – the softness of fur changing to prickly branches, the cold crunch of snow underfoot: then and then only will the reader believe. For you have made it with your mind. It's there. And it's real.

Spotlight on...
Ursula K. Le Guin

Between Me and My Shadow: Magic in Le Guin's Earthsea

Lucy Holland

Magic is not only real, but *powerful*.

I was fourteen years old when I realised this, tucked up in my room, with the floppy Puffin edition of *The Earthsea Quartet* by Ursula K. Le Guin open on my knees. I had always loved fantasy, and was certainly no stranger to magic – that urgent, mysterious force underpinning the genre. I had watched Susan wielding the Mark of Fola in Garner's *The Moon of Gomrath*. I had marvelled at the Book of Gramarye in Cooper's *The Dark is Rising*. From Robin Jarvis to Robin Hobb via Terry Pratchett, I had seen spells, sorcery, curses and conjuring. I thought I knew what magic was. I thought I knew what it could do. I was wholly unprepared for Earthsea and the power its magic would exert over me.

The various roles of magic within the novels are the pillars which support Earthsea as a fantastical literary construct. Under a critical eye, Le Guin's magic reveals itself to be multi-faceted and intersectional. It means more than charms and weather work, although both are within a wizard's remit. Magic in Earthsea is also a means of understanding the self. It is the driving force of human creativity. It is *life*. Perhaps therein lies the power that so bound me as a young reader.

We encounter these roles throughout Le Guin's first three Earthsea books, until we reach *Tehanu*. Published in 1990, almost twenty years after its predecessor, *The Farthest Shore*, this fourth novel undergoes a tonal shift, seeing 'men's magic' taking a back seat in order for the author to address the adjacent and ever-pressing question of gender. 'Weak as women's magic, wicked as women's magic'[1] is a phrase oft-repeated among the people of Earthsea – we first encounter it on page sixteen of *A Wizard of Earthsea* – and feminist readers will inevitably feel the need to have the nature of women's magic unpacked. What form it takes, what impact it has, and how it fits into Earthsea's wider magical philosophy.

Magic in fantasy tends to affect social hierarchy, leading to imbalances of power. We are used to seeing arcane oligar-

---

1   Ursula K. Le Guin, *A Wizard of Earthsea* in *The Earthsea Quartet* (Puffin, 1993), p. 16. Subsequent references are to this edition.

chies dominating common folk. But Roke Island, where Le Guin's wizards earn their staffs, does not wield undue political influence. Instead, mages hone their magical skills in service of the people among whom they live and work. This makes Earthsea a rare and fascinating example of true integration. And integration is very much the theme of this piece. We have integration of magic and society; magic and selfhood; magic and creativity; magic and gender. These all come together in Le Guin's final Earthsea novel, *The Other Wind*, where we see magic in a spiritual role, as a force able to alter the rules of life and death.

Magic as Occupation

Le Guin's first Earthsea novel, *A Wizard of Earthsea*, introduces us to magic in its simplest definition. To the inhabitants of the Archipelago, it is a familiar and practical skill which eases necessary tasks, and fits seamlessly into the wider social structure. So well incorporated is magic into Archipelagan society that its absence from the Kargish Lands fosters cultural prejudice and misunderstanding. After graduating, Le Guin's wizards find respected positions in the community. 'The uses of magic are as needful to their people as bread',[2] and among the general populace, a mage is valued far more for their ability to ward a boat, or cure a goat's infected teats, than for their ability to work great sorceries. Raised a shepherd, Ged, the titular wizard,

---

2   Ursula K. Le Guin, *The Farthest Shore* in *The Earthsea Quartet* (Puffin, 1993), p.314. Subsequent references are to this edition.

is taught to use his magic modestly. In this, Le Guin shows us magic as utility, as occupation. It is a skill, seen as a tool of everyday life rather than one of oppression.

In a good fantasy novel, magic should feel like an essential and organic component. As readers, we need to believe that it has arisen naturally, that it belongs in the world the same way people do, or mountains and seas. Such a powerful force becomes intersectional, meaning it cannot be separated from social structures such as politics and economics. This manifests culturally in Earthsea. Just as humans are distinct from one another, with different languages and practices, so too does magic behave differently depending on what part of the world a mage is in. 'Rules change in the Reaches,' is a common saying.[3] 'There are good spells I learned on Roke that have no power here,'[4] Ged's friend, Vetch, explains, as they travel into the outermost east where the fish 'do not know their own names'.[5]

The power that resides in naming, and in truth, gives Le Guin's magic an inherent honesty. While Ged can and does work illusions, he explains that the illusion of a meat pie, for instance, is no substitute for the truth of one: 'We can make it odorous, and savourous, and even filling, but it remains a word'.[6] Unlike light, one of the great powers which exists 'in itself', beyond the needs of humankind, illusion 'fools the

---

3   Le Guin, *A Wizard of Earthsea*, p.147.

4   Ibid.

5   Ibid., p.166.

6   Ibid., p.150.

stomach and gives no strength to the hungry man'.[7] There is a difference, Le Guin is saying, between word and truth, between the necessities of existence and existence itself. Illusion has its uses, but the greatest mastery resides in a mage's ability to 'summon a thing that is not there at all, to call it by speaking its true name'.[8]

As we will see, the knowledge of naming is another of magic's vital roles, bound up in archetypes and ideas of selfhood. It is a force which enables us to claim responsibility for our lives, deaths, and for the world that shapes us. This aspect of magic sits at the heart of Earthsea's defining philosophy, and guides Ged's journey as both mage and man.

Magic as Self-knowing

Even now, I flinch at typing *Ged* – so strongly was I affected by Le Guin's instruction to guard a True Name. As a teenager, I forbade my sister from reading the book, and only ever used *Sparrowhawk* to refer to its protagonist. To this day, it irks me whenever someone calls my name loudly in public, bawling out what should be held close. Whether this feeling is due to the influence of Earthsea on an impressionable young mind, there is no doubt that Le Guin's exploration of naming struck me deeply, so deeply that it put me under a geas. I could not speak Ged's name aloud – *for years*. Doing so, I felt, would give away the book's power. Or at least the power it had over me.

---

7   Ibid.

8   Ibid.

No other magic system – the term 'system' does not feel quite right here – has affected me so profoundly. I suspect it is due to the archetypal nature of Le Guin's magic. Fantasy is built on archetypes. The Jungian journey of self-discovery forms the basis of the hero's journey, a version of which appears in almost every fantasy novel. But *A Wizard of Earthsea* makes it explicit. Ged must actively reclaim his shadow self, calling it by his own name, in order to become whole. This integration forms the climax of the book. There are no grand battles here, or elaborate wizardry. Only a man and his friend in a boat sailing a vast cold sea. The ocean is symbolic of the Unconscious; it is impossible to ignore this fact when Ged himself recognises that the shadow's power is lessened upon the water – upon the sea of Self, as it were. 'At least he could grip the thing even as it gripped him,' he thinks, foreshadowing the very act of union which saves him.[9]

No grand battles, I say, but what battlefield is grander than that of the self? The very same place where Frodo fought to remain free of the Ring's influence. The same arena in which Aragorn grappled with his birthright. One might not call Ged's act of naming elaborate wizardry, and yet it is intensely magical. It is an exercise of the power that comes with knowing and accepting one's entire nature.

Similarly, Tenar's reclamation of her True Name in *The Tombs of Atuan* is the key to defeating the Nameless Ones, dark powers to which she was given as a child. Of Kossil, the cold and controlling high priestess, Ged says, 'she prowls

---

9   Ibid., p.125.

these caverns as she prowls the labyrinth of her own self,' and thereby gives us the very definition of the Nameless Ones.[10] They are no easily labelled shadow demons. Rather – like Ged's own shadow – they are psychological beings, symbolic of the ruin that results from ignorance of selfhood. In the Kargish Lands, where magic is taboo, the Nameless Ones can thrive. It is the magic of naming that Ged brings with him into the darkness, which enables their defeat. 'All things have a name,' his master, Ogion, tells him, and it is a lesson Ged has learned well.[11] Unlike Tenar, Kossil – without her True Name – has no hope of finding her way through the labyrinth of self. She has no magical power of which to speak.

Even Le Guin's geography encourages the idea of magic-as-selfhood. Making Earthsea an archipelago – a series of islands, *selves* among a great water – implies that the world's self is also fractured. The quest to reunify the world forms the plot of *The Farthest Shore*, which sees a prophesied king restored to a throne long empty, echoing Aragorn's unification of the world of men. Magic – or its dwindling – takes a central role in this novel. And herein lies yet another facet of it.

Magic as Creative Force

The waning of magic in *The Farthest Shore* is a waning of human creative power, and Le Guin explores the negative social effects

---

10   Ursula K. Le Guin, *The Tombs of Atuan* in *The Earthsea Quartet* (Puffin, 1993), p.266. Subsequent references are to this edition.

11   Le Guin, *A Wizard of Earthsea*, p.119.

of this decline. Wizards do not just lose their ability to weave spells, but craftspeople forget their crafts. Ancient songs and ritual words can no longer be recalled, leading to a withering of tradition. Ged and Arren's visit to the South Reach paints an even bleaker picture. Mass consumerism, shoddy goods and drug dens abound. The people of Lorbanery lose the secrets of silk-making and dyeing. 'Everything's grey,' Arren says.[12] All joy has effectively gone out of the world.

The 'art magic' in this book is a manifestation of ancestral skill, akin to those inherited art forms we call the intangible cultural heritage of humanity. Le Guin's addition of the word 'art' suggests that magic is an inherently creative force, and that creativity is the stuff of life. When the wall between life and death is breached, decline and stagnation is the result.

The Farthest Shore sees magic at its most globally vital. Its loss affects the whole population, plunging the world into chaos, allowing power imbalances, and facilitating the dissolution of society. This novel is also the most politically relevant; for a book published in 1973, it is a remarkable and chilling foreshadowing of the state of the creative industries today, and the wider capitalist world. The use of generative AI threatens to replace magic with sterility, far too like the blighted Earthsea. And the cause is the same: human hubris and human greed.

In Le Guin's novel, this is embodied by Cob, a dark mage who – covetous of life – seeks immortality. We have already witnessed the importance of naming. We have seen how much stronger a person becomes when they embrace their whole

---

12   Le Guin, *The Farthest Shore*, p.379.

self. But therein lies a new danger. For 'to be oneself is a rare thing, and a great one. To be oneself forever, is that not greater still?'[13] The desire to '*let the world rot so long as I can live*' is the destructive egoism that drives Cob, a man who considers himself to be 'above nature'.[14]

Does this terrifying narcissism sound familiar? Again, Le Guin has a finger on the pulse of reality. Magic – like human creativity – is movement, just as 'the Balance is not a stillness' but 'an eternal becoming'.[15] The idea of preserving Balance, or Equilibrium, will not be new to fantasy readers. It is central to the archetypal struggle between Good and Evil, and, as always, it is humans who have the most difficulty with it. 'We must *learn* to do what the leaf and the whale and the wind do of their own nature. We must learn to keep the balance. Having intelligence, we must not act in ignorance. Having choice, we must not act without responsibility.'[16] Such a statement could as easily be applied to a world experiencing unmitigated climate change as to a world being drained of magic. Both grow from the same avaricious root. The cure? Le Guin draws a powerful link between creativity and health; the health of our own selfhood and of the planet's.

It is both ironic and deeply *right* that Ged gives every drop of his magic to close the breach through which magic is being lost. I was young when I first read the novel, and experienced a young

13   Ibid., p.422.

14   Ibid.

15   Ibid., p.423.

16   Ibid., p.361.

person's visceral response: disappointment. I loved Ged the Archmage just as I had loved Ged the ambitious student wizard. I did not know who he would be without his magic – and neither does he, at first. But painful though this change is, he possesses the wisdom to recognise the necessity of it: 'I know that there is only one power worth having. And that is the power, not to take, but to accept.'[17] This declaration resonates with a later one from a very different source: the witch woman, Moss. In pointing out the difference between men's power and women's power, she says to Tenar in *Tehanu*, 'A man gives out, dearie. A woman takes in.'[18] Ged's resolution to *accept* sows the seeds of his next and final form. And with it comes yet another depiction of magic.

Magic as an Expression of Gender

In *Tehanu*, we find a feminist discussion of gender and power, for the abused girl-child, Therru, shares the focus of the story with Ged's loss of magic; a force upon which his understanding of manhood and masculinity relies. The novel opens on troubled times. Events in *The Farthest Shore* have led to Gont's social decline. Young men have turned to banditry. Women no longer feel safe alone out of doors. The first scene is a group of women dealing with the aftermath of the physical and sexual abuse of a child, which hits as hard as intended. There is much discussion of disability and worth, expressed in the context of a broader

---

17   Ibid., p.424.

18   Ursula K. Le Guin, *Tehanu* in *The Earthsea Quartet* (Puffin, 1993) p.572. Subsequent references are to this edition.

rumination on women's roles as reproductive objects in the eyes of the Patriarchy. Women stand at the centre of this book, just as they were confined to the fringes of previous Earthsea novels.

We are finally allowed to see a little of the so-called 'weak' women's magic in Moss, the local witch. 'When you had a man, Moss, did you have to give up your power?' Tenar asks as they are discussing Ged's lifelong celibacy. 'Not a bit of it,' Moss replies.[19] Unlike the celibate wizards, she is a sexually mature and liberated woman, whose power does not appear to be contingent on an assumed gendered behaviour. For men, however, magic is masculinity. The loss of it equates to emasculation, and engenders feelings of shame in Ged until he learns – with Tenar's help – to transcend them. 'All the greatness of men is founded on shame, made out of it,'[20] he realises, seeing magic as a tool of patriarchy for the first time. Perhaps seeing the Patriarchy itself for the first time, and the damage it does to those who live under its yoke.

Thus Le Guin reveals Roke Island's core failure: teaching boys there is only one kind of male power, which resides exclusively outside the home, beyond the washing of dishes and the rearing of children. And then to bind the definition of masculine identity to that power. Ogion the Silent, Ged's old master, knows this. 'I have what you lack,'[21] he tells the boy in *A Wizard of Earthsea*, hoping to keep Ged under his tutelage in rural Gont, far from the patriarchal sway of Roke.

19   Le Guin, *Tehanu*, p.572.

20   Ibid., p.666.

21   Le Guin, *A Wizard of Earthsea*, p.32.

Three books later, Ged yields up his role as dispenser of wisdom to Tenar, who reveals to him – through her experience of womanhood – that his loss is in truth a gain. Both in maturity and understanding. Women's magic is labelled 'wicked' because it is unbound by gendered convention, and has the ability to show men that turning their backs on patriarchy is *not* an emasculation. 'Why are men *afraid* of women?' Tenar asks Ged during this key conversation. 'If your strength is only the other's weakness, you live in fear,' Ged replies. To which Tenar answers, 'Yes; but women seem to fear their own strength, to be afraid of themselves.'[22] This is, of course, one of the keystones of patriarchy, upon which the whole edifice depends.

After Ged has helped to rescue her from the Nameless Ones, Tenar makes an important choice: she turns her back on the life offered by Ogion – to study magic with him – and instead becomes a wife and mother. It could be argued that just as wizards must remain celibate to practise magic, so must women reject motherhood. It is a dynamic likely to cause debate, for it is true that wife-and-mother Tenar cannot work the same witch charms as Moss. But does that mean she is an unmagical being? As we have seen, Tenar's magic is not expressed in magery, but in wisdom gained from lived experience. It is through her care and understanding of selfhood that both Ged and Therru are healed, the latter coming into the knowledge of her true self as one of the dragon people. And as we will see in Le Guin's final Earthsea novel, the rule of celibacy for wizards is abandoned as part of a larger evolutionary movement towards equality.

---

22   Le Guin, *Tehanu*, p.665.

Magic as Cause and Cure

The change that begins in *The Farthest Shore* and continues in *Tehanu* culminates in *The Other Wind*. Magic is, once again, at the centre of this change, and is revealed to be the force which created the Dry Land, preventing the dead from being reborn. The patriarchal structures upheld as wisdom on Roke are finally recognised as a corruption of nature. Men have used the art magic as a means to live beyond death, and in so doing, have broken the cycle of rebirth. The rebalancing begins with the dragon woman, Irian, coming to Roke. The celibate Master Patterner falls in love with her. A further three women visit the Immanent Grove, breaching Roke's innermost sanctum. For as the oppression of women's magic helped break the spiritual cycle, so will its liberation heal it.

We are, in short, witnessing the birth of Earthsea's feminism, and the world that greets us at the end of the novel – with a foreign queen in a position of power – heralds a new era for the women of Earthsea, and a new era for magic too. When the houses 'built wrong' are rebuilt, 'who will come in the doors' asks the Doorkeeper.[23] Who indeed? It is women's knowledge and power that guides the wizards of Roke towards the truth, and – delightfully – there are references to Tenar and Ged both 'keeping the house' in this novel.

What insights, then, can we take away from Earthsea's complex, intersectional magic? Critics argue that the system is 'overpowered', that the lack of explanation around its limits

---

23   Ursula K. Le Guin, *The Other Wind* (Orion, 2002) p.232.

creates plot and worldbuilding issues within the text. On one hand, it *is* overpowered – look at the command wielded by those who possess the knowledge of both self and world. But the magic of Earthsea cannot be viewed in terms of a 'system'. It will not be compressed into a Dungeons & Dragons-style summary of what it can and cannot do.

Le Guin shows us the potential of magic to be far more than hocus-pocus. Like its wielder, Ged, it evolves. She uses it to articulate robust concerns, from gender and selfhood to the very nature of reality. How is one to go about itemising such a force? How can you set limits on essential human expression? The beauty and depth of Le Guin's magic resides in the magnificent variety of its roles, which allow each other space to breathe. It is, in many ways, ineffable; a power able to represent all that we are and hope to say about existence. No wonder, then, that it bound me so strongly as a young person, and has remained with me as a writer, influencing much of my own creative work.

The closest Le Guin comes to a panoptic definition of magic – pulling its various roles together – is through Ged's description of it as being 'one in source and end'. Cyclical. As we have seen, power is human craft. It is the wisdom inherent in nature. It is a thing's True Name. All these expressions combine to form the 'syllables of the great word that is very slowly spoken by the shining of the stars'.[24]

---

24   Le Guin, *A Wizard of Earthsea*, p.151.

Sources

What Can Tolkien's Creative Process Teach a Writer Today?

Carpenter, Humphrey, *J.R.R. Tolkien The Authorised Biography* (George Allen and Unwin (Publishers) Ltd, 1977)

Duriez, Colin, *J.R.R. Tolkien and C.S. Lewis* (Sutton Publishing Ltd, 2003)

Flieger, Verlyn & Douglas A. Anderson (eds), *Tolkien on Fairy Stories* (HarperCollins, 2014)

Garth, John, *Tolkien and the Great War* (HarperCollins, 2003)

Haber, Karen (ed.), *Meditations on Middle-Earth* (Earthlight, 2002)

Shippey, Tom, *J.R.R. Tolkien Author of the Century* (HarperCollins, 2000)

Shippey, Tom, *The Road to Middle-Earth* (HarperCollins, 2005)

Tolkien, J.R.R., *The Monsters and the Critics and other essays* (HarperCollins, 2006)

Tolkien, J.R.R., *The Hobbit* (George Allen and Unwin (Publishers) Ltd, 1937)

Tolkien, J.R.R., *The Lord of the Rings* (George Allen and Unwin (Publishers) Ltd, 1966)

Tolkien, J.R.R., *Sir Gawain and the Green Knight, Pearl, and Sir Orfeo* (HarperCollins, 1995)

Zaleski, Philip & Carol Zaleski, *The Fellowship* (Farrar, Straus and Giroux, 2016)

On the Nature of Dragons

Bruce, Scott G., *The Penguin Book of Dragons* (Penguin Classics, 2022)

Funke, Cornelia, *How to Train Your Dragon* (Hodder Children's Books, 2003)

Guillain, Charlotte, *Dragons* (Heinmann/Raintree, 2010)

Heaney, Seamus (trans.), *Beowulf: Bilingual Edition* (Faber, 1999)

Knighton, Andrew, *The Executioner's Blade* (Northodox Press Ltd, 2024)

Lowachee, Karin, *The Mountain Crown* (Solaris, 2024)

Malam, John, *Dragons* (QED, 2009)

McCaffery, Anne, *Dragonflight* (Ballantine Books, 1968)

McKinley, Robin, *The Hero and the Crown* (William Morrow, 1984)

Miller, Carey, *Mysteries of the Unknown* (Usborne Publishing Ltd, 1977)

Novik, Naomi, *His Majesty's Dragon/Temeraire* (Del Rey & Voyager, 2006)

O'Connor, William, *Dracopedia Field Guide* (Impact, 2019)

Paolini, Christopher, *Eragon* (Alfred A. Knopf, 2003)

Parker, Sarah A., *When the Moon Hatched* (Harper Voyager, 2024)

Peebles, Alice, *Demons and Dragons* (Hungry Tomato, 2015)

Pratchett, Terry, *Guards! Guards!* (Gollancz, 1989)

Simpson, Jacqueline, *British Dragons* (Batsford, 1980)

Tolkien, J.R.R., *The Hobbit* (George Allen & Unwin, 1937)

Vicarious Dreams: Fantasy and Tie-in Fiction

Strachan, Richard, *Warcry Catacombs: Blood of the Everchosen* (Black Library, 2020)

Strachan, Richard, *The End of Enlightenment* (Black Library, 2021)

Strachan, Richard, *Hallowed Ground* (Black Library, 2022)

Strachan, Richard, *The Vulture Lord* (Black Library, 2022)

Strachan, Richard, *Temple of Silence* (Black Library, 2023)

Strachan, Richard, *Blightslayer* (Black Library, 2023)

The Door in the Mound

Aiken, Joan, *The Way to Write for Children* (St Martin's Press, 1982)

Chesterton, G.K., 'On Household Gods and Goblins' in *The Coloured Lands* (Sheed & Ward, 1938)

Deonn, Tracy, *Legendborn* (Simon & Schuster, 2020)

Fisher, Catherine, *The Clockwork Crow* (Firefly Press, 2018)

Garner, Alan, *Elidor* (Collins, 1965)

Garner, Alan, *Treacle Walker* (Fourth Estate, 2021)

Hardinge, Frances, *Deeplight* (Macmillan, 2019)

Ho-Yen, Polly, *The Last Dragon* (Knights Of, 2024)

Lewis, C.S., *The Lion, the Witch and the Wardrobe* (Puffin Books, 1973)

Lewis, C.S., *The Silver Chair* (Collins & Sons, 1990)

Lewis, C.S., 'On Three Ways of Writing for Children' in *On Stories and Other Essays on Literature*, ed. Walter Hooper (Harcourt, 1982)

Lurie, Alison, *Don't Tell The Grown-ups: Subversive Children's Literature* (Bloomsbury, 1990)

Potter, Beatrix, *The Tale of Mr Tod* (Frederick Warne & Co. Ltd, 1912)

Pullman, Philip, *The Amber Spyglass* (Alfred A Knopf, 2000)

Rundell, Katherine, *Why You Should Read Children's Books, Even Though You Are So Old and Wise* (Bloomsbury, 2019)

Said, S.F., *Tyger* (David Fickling Books, 2022)

Tolkien, J.R.R., *The Fellowship of the Ring* (George Allen and Unwin, 1969)

Between Me and My Shadow: Magic in Le Guin's Earthsea

Le Guin, Ursula K., The Earthsea Quartet (Puffin, 1993)

Le Guin, Ursula K., The Other Wind (Orion, 2002)

Further Reading

It's become our tradition to offer recommended reading lists at the end of these volumes, and *Writing the Magic* is no exception. The eagle-eyed among you will notice that, this time, the lists are skewed heavily in favour of novels. This is not to suggest there are insufficient fantasy short stories of quality – if anything, there are too many – but simply a practical recognition of the fact that many excellent fantasy stories sadly only have a brief shelf life, and are no longer widely available. (For the same reason, a couple of novellas and novelettes have snuck into the short story list – these tend to stick around a little longer.) As always, we've limited each author to a couple of entries, although many would be worthy of more, and we've attempted to leaven the well-known with a sprinkling of largely forgotten gems. As befits the genre, an attempt has been made to represent as many subgenres of fantasy as possible, too.

This is by no means intended as an exhaustive list, and many fine novels and short stories failed to make the cut. It is our hope that it will at least provide an interesting reading list, wherever you are on your journey.

100 Fantasy Novels

1. Apuleius – *The Golden Ass* (c.160)
2. Thomas Malory – *Le Morte d'Arthur* (1485)
3. Lewis Carroll – *Alice's Adventures in Wonderland* (1865)
4. William Morris – *The Well at the World's End* (1896)
5. E. Nesbit – *Five Children and It* (1902)
6. William Hope Hodgson – *The Night Land* (1912)
7. Lord Dunsany – *The King of Elfland's Daughter* (1924)
8. Beryl Irving– *The Dawnchild* (1926)
9. Hope Mirrlees – *Lud-in-the-Mist* (1926)
10. John Masefield – *The Box of Delights* (1935)
11. J.R.R. Tolkien – *The Hobbit* (1937)
12. T.H. White – *The Sword in the Stone* (1938)
13. Enid Blyton – *The Enchanted Wood* (1939)
14. Ursula Moray Williams – *Gobbolino, The Witch's Cat* (1942)
15. Mervyn Peake – *Titus Groan* (1946)
16. C.S. Lewis – *The Lion, the Witch and the Wardrobe* (1950)
17. Amos Tutuola – *The Palm-Wine Drunkard* (1952)
18. J.R.R. Tolkien – *The Fellowship of the Ring* (1954)
19. Poul Anderson – *The Broken Sword* (1954)
20. Philippa Pearce – *Tom's Midnight Garden* (1958)
21. Alan Garner – *The Weirdstone of Brisingamen* (1960)
22. Joan Aiken – *The Wolves of Willoughby Chase* (1962)
23. Jorge Luis Borges – *Labyrinths* (1962)
24. Lloyd Alexander – *The Book of Three* (1964)
25. Manuel Mujica Lainez – *The Wandering Unicorn* (1965)
26. Alan Garner – *Elidor* (1965)
27. Mikhail Bulgakov – *The Master and Margarita* (1967)

28. Ursula K. Le Guin – *A Wizard of Earthsea* (1968)

29. Peter S. Beagle – *The Last Unicorn* (1968)

30. Anne McCaffrey – *Dragonflight* (1969)

31. Mary Stewart – *The Crystal Cave* (1970)

32. Richard Adams – *Watership Down* (1972)

33. Susan Cooper – *The Dark is Rising* (1972)

34. Michael Moorcock – *Elric of Melniboné*(1972)

35. William Goldman – *The Princess Bride* (1973)

36. Patricia A. McKillip – *The Forgotten Beasts of Eld* (1974)

37. C.J. Cherryh – *Gate of Ivrel* (1976)

38. Stephen Donaldson – *Lord Foul's Bane* (1977)

39. Walter Wangerin Jr – *The Book of the Dun Cow*(1978)

40. Tanith Lee – *Night's Master* (1978)

41. Patricia A. McKillip – *Harpist in the Wind* (1979)

42. Tim Powers – *The Drawing of the Dark* (1979)

43. Jonathan Carroll – *The Land of Laughs* (1980)

44. Gene Wolfe – *The Shadow of the Torturer* (1980)

45. Michael Moorcock – *The Warhound and the World's Pain* (1981)

46. Salman Rushdie – *Midnight's Children* (1981)

47. Steve Jackson & Ian Livingstone – *The Warlock of Firetop Mountain* (1982)

48. Raymond E. Feist – *Magician* (1982)

49. Jack Vance – *Lyonesse* (1983)

50. Marion Zimmer Bradley – *The Mists of Avalon* (1983)

51. Robert Holdstock – *Mythago Wood* (1984)

52. David Gemmell – *Legend* (1984)

53. Margaret Weis & Tracy Hickman – *Dragons of Autumn Twilight* (1984)

54. Barbara Hambly – *Dragonsbane* (1985)

55. Brian Jacques – *Redwall* (1986)

56. Katherine Kerr – *Daggerspell* (1986)

57. Diana Wynne Jones – *Howl's Moving Castle* (1986)

58. Terry Brooks – *Magic Kingdom for Sale–Sold!* (1986)

59. Ellen Kushner – *Swordspoint* (1987)

60. Helen Cresswell – *Moondial* (1987)

61. Terry Pratchett – *Mort* (1987)

62. Elizabeth Moon – *The Deed of Paksenarrion* (1989)

63. Robert Jordan – *The Eye of the World* (1990)

64. Guy Gavriel Kay – *Tigana* (1990)

65. Clive Barker – *Imajica* (1991)

66. Sheri S. Tepper – *Beauty* (1991)

67. Elizabeth Hand – *Waking the Moon* (1994)

68. Robin Hobb – *Assassin's Apprentice* (1995)

69. Philip Pullman – *Northern Lights* (1995)

70. Garth Nix – *Sabriel* (1995)

71. George R.R. Martin – *A Game of Thrones* (1996)

72. Steven Erikson – *Gardens of the Moon* (1999)

73. Lois McMaster Bujold – *The Curse of Chalion* (2001)

74. Jacqueline Carey – *Kushiel's Dart* (2001)

75. Terry Pratchett – *Night Watch* (2002)

76. Jeff VanderMeer – *Veniss Underground* (2003)

77. Susanna Clarke – *Jonathan Strange & Mr Norrell* (2004)

78. Jim Butcher – *Furies of Calderon* (2004)

79. Kate Elliott – *Spirit Gate* (2006)

80. Joe Abercrombie – *The Blade Itself* (2006)

81. Patrick Rothfuss – *The Name of the Wind* (2007)

82. Peter V. Brett – *The Painted Man* (2008)

83. Margo Lanagan – *Tender Morsels* (2008)

84. N.K. Jemisin – *The Hundred Thousand Kingdoms* (2010)

85. Brandon Sanderson – *The Way of Kings* (2010)

86. Erin Morgenstern – *The Night Circus* (2011)

87. Nnedi Okorafor – *Akata Witch* (2011)

88. B. Catling – *The Vorrh* (2012)

89. Graham Joyce – *Some Kind of Fairy Tale* (2013)

90. Frances Hardinge – *Cuckoo Song* (2014)

91. Kazuo Ishiguro – *The Buried Giant* (2015)

92. N.K. Jemisin – *The Fifth Season* (2015)

93. Tochi Onyebuchi – *Beasts Made of Night* (2017)

94. R.F. Kuang – *The Poppy War* (2018)

95. Jen Williams – *The Ninth Rain* (2018)

96. Frances Hardinge – *Deeplight* (2019)

97. Marlon James – *Black Leopard, Red Wolf* (2019)

98. Susanna Clarke – *Piranesi* (2020)

99. Shelley Parker-Chan – *She Who Became the Sun* (2021)

100. Vajra Chandrasekera – *The Saint of Bright Doors* (2023)

30 Fantasy Short Stories

1. Brothers Grimm – 'Snow-White' (1812)

2. E.T.A. Hoffman – 'The Golden Pot' (1814)

3. Hans Christian Andersen – 'The Snow Queen' (1844)

4. Willa Cather – 'The Princess Baladina' (1896)

5. Lord Dunsany – 'The Fortress Unvanquishable, Save for Sacnoth' (1908)

6. Lord Dunsany – 'The Hoard of the Gibbelins' (1911)

7. E.M. Forster – 'The Celestial Omnibus' (1911)

8. Robert E. Howard – 'Rogues in the House' (1934)

9. Robert E. Howard – 'Red Nails' (1936)

10. J.R.R. Tolkien – 'Leaf by Niggle' (1945)

11. Vladimir Nabokov – 'Signs and Symbols' (1948)

12. Jack Vance – 'Liane the Wayfarer' (1950)

13. Michael Moorcock – 'The Dreaming City' (1961)

14. Tove Jansson – 'The Last Dragon in the World' (1962)

15. Fritz Leiber – 'Ill Met in Lankhmar' (1970)

16. Larry Niven – 'The Magic Goes Away' (1976)

17. Angela Carter – 'The Snow Child' (1979)

18. C.J. Cherryh – 'The Dreamstone' (1979)

19. Elizabeth A. Lynn – The Woman Who Loved the Moon' (1979)

20. Tanith Lee – 'The Sombrus Tower' (1981)

21. Stephen King – 'The Gunslinger' (1982)

22. James P. Blaylock – 'Paper Dragons' (1985)

23. John M. Ford – 'Winter Solstice, Camelot Station' (1988)

24. Patricia A. McKillip – 'The Lady of the Skulls' (1992)

25. Victor LaValle – 'I Left My Heart in Skaftafell' (2004)

26. Daniel Abraham – 'The Cambist and Lord Iron: A Fairy Tale of Economics' (2007)

27. Ken Liu – 'The Paper Menagerie' (2011)

28. Alyssa Wong – 'Hungry Daughters of Starving Mothers' (2015)

29. Amal El-Mohtar – 'Seasons of Glass and Iron' (2016)

30. P. Djeli Clark – 'If the Martians Have Magic' (2021)

About the Authors

RJ Barker is a critically acclaimed and award-winning author of fantasy fiction. He won the 2020 British Fantasy Society (BFS) Robert Holdstock Award for Best Novel for his fourth novel, *The Bone Ships*. The award-winning Tide Child Trilogy – *The Bone Ships*, *Call of the Bone Ships* and *The Bone Ships Wake* – have been hailed as 'One of the most interesting and original fantasy worlds I've seen in years' by Adrian Tchaikovsky, and 'Brilliant' by Robin Hobb, alongside rave reviews in *Starburst*, *SFX*, and a starred review in *Booklist*: 'A unique and memorable world – harsh and brutal and full of fully realized, powerful female characters.' RJ lives in Leeds with his wife, son and a collection of questionable taxidermy, odd art, scary music and more books than they have room for. He grew up reading whatever he could get his hands on, and has always been 'that one with the book in his pocket'. Having played in rock bands before deciding he was a rubbish musician, RJ returned to his first love, fiction.

Charlotte Bond is an author, freelance editor, and podcaster. Under her own name she has written within the genres of horror and dark fantasy, but she's also worked as a ghostwriter.

She edits books for individuals and publishers, and has also contributed numerous non-fiction articles to various websites. At one point, she was a regular contributor of mostly historical and sometimes bizarre articles to *The Vintage News* website. She is a co-host of the award-winning podcast *Breaking the Glass Slipper*. Her micro collection *The Watcher in the Woods* won the British Fantasy Society's award for Best Collection in 2021. Her novellas *The Fireborne Blade* and *The Bloodless Princes* were published by Tordotcom in 2024. Most recently, her short stories have appeared in anthologies published by Flame Tree Press. She is represented by Alex Cochran.

Francesco Dimitri lives in London, where he arrived, via Rome, from the depths of Southern Italy. He published eight books in Italian before switching to English. His first Italian novel was made into a film, and his last was defined by *Il Corriere della Sera* as the sort of book from which a genre 'starts again'. His first novel in English, *The Book of Hidden Things*, has been optioned for film and TV. In fall 2026, Tor.com will publish an English translation by Sophia MacDougall of his 2008 novel *Pan*, which Italian critics called 'necessary', 'like a bomb' and 'timeless'.

Lucy Holland is an author working across the fields of history, mythology and fantasy. Her current interest lies in reimagining folk tales and Celtic myth, with a view to re-situating the stories of queer people and uncovering the complex regional histories of early medieval Britain. Her novel *Sistersong* was a finalist for both the Goldsboro Books Glass Bell Award and the British Fantasy Award for Best Novel in 2022. Her second historical fantasy, *Song of the Huntress*, was published by Pan Macmillan in 2024. Both books are set in the West Country where she lives, and were inspired by its rich local folklore and history. Since 2016, Lucy has co-hosted the British Fantasy Award-winning podcast *Breaking the Glass Slipper*, with a focus on women in speculative fiction. She has given talks and workshops at various universities and venues, including the British Library, Science Museum London, Barcelona Festival 42 and Edinburgh's Cymera Festival. Lucy created and currently leads Curtis Brown Creative's flagship Writing Fantasy course, which runs twice a year. In June 2024, she was selected by UNESCO Cities of Literature as one of the ILX10: Rising Stars of UK Writing.

Hannah Kaner is an award-nominated Northumbrian writer living in Scotland (mostly). Her Fallen Gods Trilogy is a #1 *Sunday Times* Bestseller, and her work has been published around the world in 15 languages and counting. Her career has been in digital consultancy and delivering accessible tools and services into the public sector, and she has a first class degree in English from Pembroke College, Cambridge and a MSc from Edinburgh University. She is inspired by world mythologies, angry women, speculative fiction, and the stories we tell ourselves about being human.

Katherine Langrish is the author of a number of historical fantasies for children, including the critically acclaimed trilogy

West of the Moon and *Dark Angels* (HarperCollins), and her books have been published in many countries including the USA. Katherine is the creator of the award-winning blog *Seven Miles of Steel Thistles*, which discusses folklore, fairy tales and fantasy, and she was invited in 2022 to give the annual Katharine Briggs Memorial Lecture to the Folklore Society. Her most recent publication is *From Spare Oom to War Drobe: Travels in Narnia with my nine year-old self* (Darton, Longman & Todd, 2021) and she is currently working on a YA novel.

Juliet E. McKenna is a British fantasy author living in the Cotswolds, UK. Her epic fantasy debut, *The Thief's Gamble*, began the Tales of Einarinn in 1999, followed by the Aldabreshin Compass sequence, the Chronicles of the Lescari Revolution, and the Hadrumal Crisis trilogies, fifteen novels in all. In 2015, she received the British Fantasy Society's Karl Edward Wagner Award. *The Green Man's Heir* was her first modern fantasy inspired by British folklore in 2018. *The Green Man's Quarry* won the BSFA Award for Best Novel 2023, and *The Green Man's War* followed in 2024 as the seventh title in this ongoing series. Her 2023 novel *The Cleaving* is a female-centred retelling of the story of King Arthur, while her shorter fiction includes forays into dark fantasy, steampunk, science fiction and shared-world projects. She has served as a judge for the James White Award, the Aeon Award, the Arthur C. Clarke Award and the World Fantasy Awards. She reviews SF&Fantasy, blogs on book trade issues, and teaches creative writing as and when she is invited. For more, visit www.julietemckenna.com.

Jeff Noon was born in Manchester, England. He trained in the visual arts and was active on the post-punk music scene before becoming a playwright, and then a novelist. His science fiction books include *Vurt* (Arthur C. Clarke Award), *Pollen, Automated Alice, Falling Out of Cars*, and a collection of stories called *Pixel Juice*. He has written two crime novels, *Slow Motion Ghosts* and *House with no Doors*. The four Nyquist Mysteries (*A Man of Shadows, The Body Library, Creeping Jenny* and *Within Without*) explore the shifting intersections between SF and crime. His latest books are *Gogmagog* and *Ludluda*, two alternative-world fantasy novels created in collaboration with Steve Beard. X: @jeffnoon.

Alex Pheby is the award-winning and internationally bestselling writer of *Grace, Playthings, Lucia*, and the Cities of Weft trilogy.

Kritika H. Rao is a speculative fiction author, whose works include *The Surviving Sky* and *The Legend of Meneka*. Kritika has lived in India, Australia, Canada, and the Sultanate of Oman, and her stories are influenced by her lived experiences. Themes of self vs the world, identity, and the nature of consciousness inevitably make their way into her work. When she is not writing, she is probably making lists. She drops in and out of social media; you might catch her on Instagram @KritikaHRao. Visit her online at www.kritikahrao.com.

Richard Strachan lives in Edinburgh. His short fiction has been published in magazines like *Interzone, The Dark, Weird*

Horror, New Writing Scotland and *The Lonely Crowd*. His novel *The Unrecovered* was published by Raven Books in 2025.

Jen Williams is a writer from London currently living in Bristol with her partner and a dramatically fluffy cat. A fan of grisly fairy tales since her youth, Jen has gone on to write dark, unsettling horror thrillers with strong female leads and character-driven fantasy novels with plenty of adventure and magic. The Winnowing Flame trilogy twice won the British Fantasy Award for best novel, and the first volume of the Talon Duology, *Talonsister*, picked up the same award in 2024. She is partially responsible for the creation of the long-running social event Super Relaxed Fantasy Club, and her first thriller, *Dog Rose Dirt*, was optioned for television by Gaumont. 2025 will see the release of her first YA fantasy novel, *The Sleepless*. When not writing books, Jen enjoys scary movies, tabletop roleplaying games and the sort of video games where you can get dumped by a sexy elf. She also works as a freelance copywriter and illustrator.

J.L. Worrad is the author of the fantasy novels *Pennyblade* and *The Keep Within*, published by Titan Books, and the science fiction novel *Feral Space*, published by Castrum Press. He has a blog at jamesworrad.com. He lives in Leicester, UK.

About the Editors

Dan Coxon is a finalist for the World Fantasy Awards (for *Heartwood: A Mythago Wood Anthology*) and has won two British Fantasy Awards (for *Writing the Uncanny* and *Writing the Future*, both co-edited with Richard V. Hirst). He has been shortlisted for the British Fantasy Awards a total of eight times, and was a finalist for the Shirley Jackson Awards. In October 2025 his anthology of haunted house stories, *Unquiet Guests*, will be published by Dead Ink Books. His second short story collection, *Come Sing for the Harrowing*, will be reissued by CLASH Books in April 2026.

Richard V. Hirst is a writer and editor from Preston. His writing has been published in *The Guardian*, the *Big Issue*, *Time Out* and others.

Also in the *Writing the...* series:

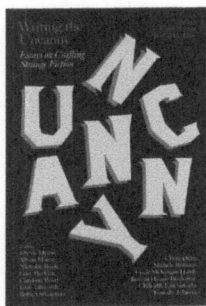

Writing the Uncanny

From M.R. James to Shirley Jackson, the Uncanny has long provided fertile ground for writers – and recent years have seen a notable resurgence in both literature and film. But how does the Uncanny work? What can a writer do to ensure their fiction haunts the reader's imagination?

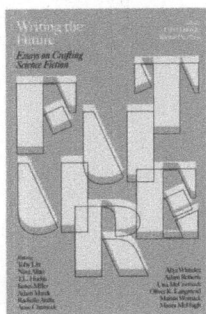

Writing the Future

Science fiction was a defining genre of the postwar era, and its current boom across books, film and TV shows no sign of slowing. Space ships, time travel, aliens and artificial intelligence continue to obsess us, and dreams of the apocalypse haunt our own post-pandemic age. But what is it that compels writers to imagine the future?

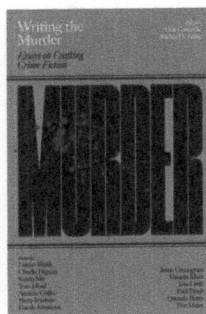

Writing the Murder

From the macabre tales of Edgar Allan Poe through to the locked-room mysteries of the Golden Age, to the many faces of modern crime fiction and the explosion of true crime, writers have always explored the most taboo of human transgressions: the taking of a life. What is it about murder that has fascinated us for so long? And what is it about crimes of this nature that make for such compelling fiction?

About Dead Ink

Dead Ink is a publisher of bold new fiction based in Liverpool. We're an Arts Council England National Portfolio Organisation.

If you would like to keep up to date with what we're up to, check out our website and join our mailing list.

www.deadinkbooks.com | @deadinkbooks